Dyslexic Suʞcess

Tod Megibow

RED LEAD PRESS
PITTSBURGH, PENNSYLVANIA 15222

The contents of this work including, but not limited to, the accuracy of events, people, and places depicted; opinions expressed; permission to use previously published materials included; and any advice given or actions advocated are solely the responsibility of the author, who assumes all liability for said work and indemnifies the publisher against any claims stemming from publication of the work.

All Rights Reserved
Copyright © 2012 by Tod Megibow

No part of this book may be reproduced or transmitted, downloaded, distributed, reverse engineered, or stored in or introduced into any information storage and retrieval system, in any form or by any means, including photocopying and recording, whether electronic or mechanical, now known or hereinafter invented without permission in writing from the publisher.

Red Lead Press
701 Smithfield Street
Pittsburgh, PA 15222
Visit our website at *www.redleadbooks.com*

ISBN: 978-1-4349-6651-3
eISBN: 978-1-4349-2628-9

DEDICATION

To Rachel who inherited my dyslexia,
and Aaron who did not.
The two of you are the measure of
my success.
Love,
Dad
July 4, 2010

Thanks to Deborah Jane for her editing skills.
You are my de facto sister and my quasi partner in the practice.

This work is entirely fictional. Any similarity to real life is purely unintended and coincidental. This material is copy writed. It may not be used without the express consent of the author.

Chapter 1

"He can put a lip lock on my love muscle!"

"Who?" Kurt asked.

"That vertically challenged obese bastard in the robe, who's having an incestuous relationship with is mother. That's who!"

"Wa?"

"That short fat mother-fucker behind the bench. That's who!"

"Isn't it amazing how quickly a witness can flip-flop on you," Kurt grumbled.

"Even when you've cocked and locked them the day before trial."

"Flip-flop, hell!" I answered.

"What really amazed me was how Simms sensed that they were going to, even before they testified."

"I wondered why Simms had that shit-eatin' grin on his face after your opening statement. Now I know why." Kurt had that beer: 30 look on his face.

"Beer, Kurt?"

Dejectedly he responded, "Sure, can't dance and it's too wet to plow."

A stop at Kurt's favorite watering hole, the local Elks club, was the obvious choice. A double Dewar's for me, a beer or six for him. The drinks wouldn't change the outcome, but they would ease the pain.

"Meet you there in a couple minutes." I said, "I've got to run by the office, return a few phone calls and bark a few orders."

No sense in calling Big Mama, I thought. She had watched the entire trial on local public access. Every night when I returned home, she gave me her impressions. She got the verdict the instant I did. At least when I got home tonight I wouldn't have the pain of reporting the verdict. She never gave me any grief when I came home with the aroma of Scotch on my breath after a shattering loss. She was a great partner. The only absolutely correct decision I had made in the last ten years was asking her to marry me.

"And the biggest mistake you made in the last ten years was accepting." I always told her. She almost always smiled back. Time, three kids and a growing practice had changed the lines on our faces and our figures, but not our relationship. If life was normally topsy-turvy, life with a dyslexic New York Jewish lawyer transplanted to Western Kentucky was a Yiddish comedy written in Sanskrit.

Getting into my car, at the courthouse parking lot, I saw Sissy's parents coming towards me. I knew what was coming. The post verdict assault alleging my incompetence. Someone had to take the fall and if Sissy was innocent, then it was obviously my fault that she was convicted. 'Mr. Mills, what went wrong? Why didn't you do such-and-such? Why didn't you do this or that?' I was in no mood for it. No matter what I said, there were sure to be a dozen more questions generated by each answer. Each question more venomously accusing me of further incompetence. I prepared for the onslaught.

"Mr. Mills, we just wanted you to know that we thought you done a real fine job o' defendin' Sissy." Her father, John Gilbert said. They were poor folks, or po'fok, as they said in western most Kentucky. Her mother tried to hold back the tears, albeit unsuccessfully. She had stood by her daughter in the face of overwhelming evidence. The evidence she told me she still found hard to believe.

"Sir, thank both of you very much. This is a trial that will wake me up in the middle of the night for quite some time. Please make an appointment to see me in the next couple of days and we can discuss the appeal. As you can tell, I'm beyond exhausted and," I paused.

Sissy's dad interrupted, "We just wanted to thank you. We know you done your best, even when the case kept getting worse."

There wasn't more to say. Worn out from the week long trial, I skipped the office and went straight to the Dewar's.

CHAPTER 2

Elks Clubs, Moose Clubs, and any club that has an antler or animal in its emblem is by its very nature generic. Booze and bullshit. This one was packed with the usual gaggle of geese hunters, fresh off the hunting reserve. It was goose season and no self-respecting man would be anywhere other than a goose pit at 3:00 a.m. Goose hunters got drunk in the late afternoon and stayed up all night to start hunting in the early morning in freezing goose pits. A right of passage I had decided to Passover. None of them were sensitive to the criminal defense lawyer's plight or our fight for due process and the rights of the falsely accused. I expected little if any sympathy from them now, and got even less. After all, most of them had predicted a conviction.

"Lost another one, 'eh counselor?" The first volley.

"Hell, he don't care. He gets paid and gets to walk out o' the courtroom whether he wins or loses." A second shot from a hunter at a corner table.

"Nice try counselor." Another.

I turned to acknowledge the disingenuous remarks and saw Kurt sitting in another corner nursing a beer and a shot.

"Come on over here and get away from those assholes," he said loudly enough for them to hear. He signaled to the bartender, Jenny, "Give my man here what he needs."

"Hell, Kurt, what I need is sleep and a couple of weeks with the kids and Big Mama. On second thought, you take the kids and I'll take the wife."

"Or visa versa counselor." Kurt had always thought that Big Mama, my diminutive term for my wife - because she never weighed more than ninety-eight pounds dripping wet in an Eskimo's parka, was a good looker. He was right, and he never missed an opportunity to let me know it. While Kurt had dated a number of good-to-gorgeous looking women, and had come close to getting married once, he never took the leap. I never asked, and he never told me what happened that one time. I always thought that like me, he was married to his work. It didn't take me long after beginning to practice law to learn that the law was a jealous mistress – demanding all and returning little.

"Sissy took the verdict pretty well, didn't she?"

"Yea Kurt, she was a real trooper. On the other hand, I'll bet if we stuck a thermometer up his honor's derriere it would have read minus thirty-two degrees."

"Fahrenheit or Celsius?"

"Kelvin."

"What now? Appeal?" Kurt asked. He knew the answer.

"Yea. The family doesn't have the money to hire me to do the appeal. I know some of the boys and girls in Frankfort who do the public defender appellate work. I think we have at least one hot issue, maybe two. If I can convince them that they are hot then we can get Sissy one of the better appellate attorneys and stand a better chance of a reversal. She got more than twenty years so we've only got one shot on appeal."

Kentucky's appellate system gave you two shots on appeal if you were sentenced to less than twenty years. First, to The Court of Appeals, then to The Supreme Court on a motion for discretionary review. If you got more than twenty years you had one chance with the Supreme Court. One shot with the magnificent seven. Seven Justices that never saw a conviction they didn't like and want to affirm.

"Sissy has one shot on appeal." I mumbled and chuckled at the irony. One shot was all it had taken to kill Walker. Who'd a thunk it? I thought to myself. Shot once with a .25 cal. The damn bullet gets lucky, if you can call that luck, hits Walker's collarbone, takes a ninety degree turn downward, and severs his aorta and he bleed out. There wasn't a goose hunter in here that wouldn't have been proud of that shot.

The people at the next table in the bar quieted down, and tried to look occupied. Trying to catch a word or two of our conversation. Then they could tell the good ole boys at the 5:00 a.m. breakfast club that they had heard us say "such and such," and appear to be "in-the-know." Kurt and I glanced at each other.

"Billiards?" I asked.

"Got your ass kicked in court and now you want to kick mine?"

"Ass kicked is right." Three prosecutors at trial and we stood a chance? Two top prosecutors and a judge up for re-election, doing his best Nixon "law and order schpiel." Sissy's case was not a high profile case. It was a run of the mill trailer trash bar shooting. Why had the media grabbed onto it?

"You think the judge got the cable company to cover the trial to help his re-election?" Kurt asked rhetorically, then getting up and smirking his own agreement. I flipped a dime. Kurt lost. He racked. With two fingers I signaled Jenny for two more drinks. I broke and ran six balls. One victory today, albeit Pyrrhic, would be nice.

"Product of a misspent youth, Kurt," referring to my time spent as a teenager in New York City's poolrooms. It was a tough time back then. Going to a private all boys' school. Coming home with less than mediocre grades, and getting the crap beaten out of me for it. It never ceased to amaze me how my father thought that beating me would improve my study habits. They hadn't had the tests run yet that showed I was dyslexic. The tests that showed I was ADD-RT would come much later.

"Oh, yea, Dad, I'll study a lot harder," I thought to myself as the blows landed. "Now I understand this motivational technique." Next semester, same grades, same beating. It was only when I got away from the beatings and went to college to keep my 2-S draft deferment, and avoid "Bullet's 101" at the University of Vietnam, that I started to make decent grades.

"Your shot counselor." Kurt was not well pleased. He had pocketed three balls, left me with an easy shot on my last ball, which set upon the eight. A piece of cake.

"Another?" I asked.

"No, I think I've had enough punishment for one day."

"Yea, me too," I replied.

I fired down the last of the Dewar's, said adieu to Kurt and Jenny and headed out the door. Kurt ambled his six foot five, two hundred and fifty pound frame over to the bar. He, the product of a Jewish Polish mother who had survived Auschwitz and had married an African American from Philadelphia, always had a thing for bartenders. The history of his arrival in town rivaled my own. The two of us, defending a southern woman who was the antihisis of southern bell-dom.

'Ah, life in a small southern town can be so much fun for a dyslexic Yankee Jew. Could life get any busier?' I thought to myself.

Chapter 3

❖❖ Waking up to start work at 2:00 a.m. was a habit I developed in law school, especially during finals week. Now, it was always finals week. Solo practice made the 2:00 a.m. wake ups normative, and a trademark. Almost everyone in town knew I kept early hours. I had not followed in my father's footsteps into medicine because I didn't want to keep his long hours. Now I was keeping his hours, and then some. Interesting how that love-hate thing with your assailant worked out.

My most common post-verdict thought awakened me. What could I have done differently to change the result? I didn't remember if I was reliving the trial or if I was dreaming that I was back in law school taking a final in a class I had never attended. Whatever the dream, the cause was still the same. Anxiety. Anxious over what had happened, anxiety over what was going to happen, anxious over everything, and unable to control any of the variables. The cause didn't matter. The reality was the same. Two o'clock a.m., awake, and what to do? Too early to jog or walk the pure-bred pound puppy, but not too early to go to the office and play the ever popular game of catch up.

The unfortunate inevitable consequence of a week long trial was the pile of other client's work. The perquisite was a week of public visibility. Publicity never hurt a practice. In a month, the public would forget the verdict, but remember my name. While some lawyers advertised in the yellow pages, the best advertisement in a small town was always word of mouth. Something in my past that made me want to defend the 'little guy'. While the origin of this animus for authority was irrelevant, its result was personally pleasing.

The morning routine consisted of a quick shower, stopping at the 24 hour "Stop and Rob" for a large coffee and the drive to the office. The only other cars on the road at 2:00 a.m. were either leaving bars or cops trying to catch my future DUI clients. I love cops. They are my bread and butter. Whenever they came to my office for a contribution for the FOP fundraiser I gave gladly. The professionals never minded when I won a DUI. Because they assumed they knew of my big fees for defending DUI's, they knew the defendant had been punished.

Arriving at the office I noticed that the porch light, which was always left on, was out. Opening the door, everything else seemed in order. Five days of correspondence and a week of court orders to review sat on the right corner of my desk, waiting to be reviewed and moved to the left corner. Emma, my first and only staff member, had developed this dyslexic-proof system to help me keep the 'will do' from the 'done-done' material.

I had renovated the building in the early 80's during the Bob Villa renovation craze. Originally a Greek cross structure, it had been re-muddled too many times. I tried to restore it to its original architectural integrity, but at the same time make it a workable law office. The skills I had learned in my summers off from college spent working for various construction companies and welding shops came in handy. It was a project I started before I met Big Mama and one I finished right after we married. It too was a labor of love. I cherished the accomplishment and as a result it was more than an office. I lived there more than I did at home, a second Mills Manner.

Thinking back about it now, I don't remember hearing anything but breaking glass and an explosion in the back room. I didn't hear a car engine and I didn't hear a dog bark. Just the sound of breaking glass and the floor shaking like the New Madrid fault had finally given way and Western Kentucky was becoming Nevada's neighbor.

I ran to the back of the office where the noise emanated, through the reception area, down the corridor, and past the small door on the left that served as a make shift library and deposition room. The smell of gasoline and the orange glow were out of place. I turned and saw the flames pouring off of Emily's Mac. No way was I going to be able to save any of our files on her desk.

"911, what is your emergency?"

"612 North 6th Street. Fire! Firebomb!"

"What is your name, sir?"

'Fidel Fucking Castro,' I thought to myself. What the hell does it matter? My damn office is going up in flames and this babe wants to know whom the hell I am.

"Tim Mills. I'm in the office right now. Some one just threw a Molotov cocktail through my rear office window."

"We advise that you get out of the building Mr. Mills."

'We? You have a mouse in your pocket?' I thought, "And not protect all my files! No way Jose!"

She must have realized that there was no sense in arguing with a lawyer.

"The fire department is on the way, Mr. Mills. Please leave the building."

Sissy's file was safe in the trunk of my car. The main filing cabinet was locked, but it wasn't fireproof. Maybe if I stood by it with the fire extinguisher, I could save it. Where the hell was the sound of the fire truck? They probably realized it was my office and decided to take the long way and stop and get a large BBQ with slaw. Finally! The sound of fire trucks! Hoses and firemen filled the office like ham on a hog, like a collar on a dog and like stink on shit. And here I thought I was up a creek without a paddle, both oars broke and couldn't swim a stroke.

"No doubt about it Tim. It's definitely arson." It had been two hours since the chief and the fire trucks had arrived and put the fire out.

"No shit Sherlock." I muttered to myself, " I was here when the whole thing started. I told the 911 operator I smelled gasoline."

"All well and good counselor, but you know you're no expert on fires. You know we have to have proof. One of those things you lawyers require of us in court."

'Great!' I thought. My entire office almost goes up in a minute and this guy is giving me a primer on procedural criminal law and the burden of proof.

The fire chief was a typical city employee. A perfect example of the Peter Principle. The chief knew someone way back when, or knew something about someone way back when, and had gotten promoted to the point where he was above his level of competency.

"Who do you suspect, counselor?"

'Great!' First he reminds me of my job, and now he wants me to do his. Better I keep my wise-ass comments to myself and just answer his questions.

"Don't know chief, could have been anybody."

"Including you, counselor," he said smugly.

"Sure chief, just my style. Rebuild an old, small, historic building according to the historical, or hysterical code- if you will, put more money in it than I can insure it or re-sell it for, and then torch it. Makes sense to me Chief." I was as much in the mood for his sarcastic asides as he was mine.

"Stranger things have happened, Mr. Mills."

Oh great. Now it's Mr. Mills. What happened to the good ole boy sarcastic first name basis of "counselor?"

"Look Chief, I've had a really shitty week. I'm sorry if I pissed you off, but right now the last thing on my mind is who do I think did it. O.K.?"

"O.K., Tim, but you understand that everyone is a suspect in my line of work."

Ah, the classic Gestapo mentality. "Kill 'em all and let God sort 'em out."

"You are at the bottom of the list of suspects. You sure as hell didn't do it for the money, and you sure as hell aren't in trouble with the bar or anyone else as far as I know.

"No, Chief, I've still got a clean record with the boys in at the bar."

"Any other enemies that you can think of, Tim?"

"Well, after fourteen years of practice, I imagine there are a couple of pissed off ex-husbands, a couple of dozen "victims" I chewed up on the stand, and two or three cops that absolutely love me for what I did to them in a courtroom. And then there are the doctors, accountants and other professionals that I've sued that either did it or would kick in their pro rata share to pay the torch."

"How about the victim's family in the trial you just finished – the Walker family? I understand that they had to wand everyone outside the courtroom after they went through the metal detector at the courthouse entrance. All that security to protect you?"

He was right. More of the judge's antics – stirring shit to increase the aroma of a high profile case? Walker's family, or someone, spread the rumor that Sissy would never live through trial. Affidavits that cops had heard that Sissy was "dead-meat in a heartbeat" flowed like bourbon from Makers' Mark's brewery. I had Kurt wear his bulletproof vest and carry his 9 mm. I even put him between the courtroom audience and me in case bullets flew. We got his 9 mm in because we came in court officer's separate door.

"Counselor, are you sure I can carry this into the courtroom without getting in trouble?" Kurt had asked the first day of trial.

"No, Kurt, I'm not sure, but I'll represent you for free if the shit hits the fan." Kurt took no solace in the offer.

"Yea, Chief, that's a possibility," I said, focusing back on the fire and his original question. "The Walkers are a crazy bunch. I suppose they don't understand the theory of cognitive dissonance and can't disassociate Sissy from me."

The Chief looked at me blankly. Evidently he didn't understand the communication's theory of cognitive dissonance either. I was talking over his head but he didn't want to appear uneducated and I didn't want to take the time to explain a relatively simple theory to him.

"If there's nothing else, I've got a lot of things to do, Chief."

He nodded, and barked some orders to the fire fighters, indicating my audience with him was over. I sure had my belly full of him too.

Calls to make to get a temporary office set up, cleaning services, Emily, Kurt; the list forming in my head. I also had prayers to say for having been in the right place at the right time and for having been looked after. I wasn't the most observant Jew, but I knew when thanks were due. If yesterday had been a lousy day, today wasn't shaping up any better.

Chapter 4

"Why should the court grant you an extension to file you motion for a new trial, Mr. Mills?"

"Well, your honor," I paused, thinking to myself that the old son of a bitch was still just as cold as he was during Sissy's trial. "There was this small conflagration at my office that you may have read about. We are trying to get all of our records dried out, and seeing what we can salvage from the hard drives. There is also the problem of getting the insurance company to give me the money to buy the equipment to type up the motion." I paused, 'I'd like to give you a hard drive.' I thought. "And your honor, the Commonwealth does not oppose the motion."

Just as Ivory soap is ninety-nine and forty-four one hundredths percent pure, judges unconsciously sign orders if the opposition, and particularly the Commonwealth, agrees to them. What was his problem? I'd call his wife and pay her to 'give him some,' but he was going through a divorce. Hell, I'd pay any babe to 'give him some' if it would help his mood. But who would do him? No one's standards were that low. If they did him, it was because he had the most powerful aphrodisiac a man could have. Power! Power and money were the top two aphrodisiacs. A sense of humor was the third. He was losing the second in his divorce and never had the third.

'Besides that, you old fart, if you remember what it was like to practice law, I have more than one case going at a time,' I thought to myself. Good God if this judge could just read my mind I'd be six feet under the jail, not in it on a contempt citation.

"Very well, Mr. Mills, you have five days."

'Oh, thank you, your magnificence. How gracious of you your magnificence. Kiss my ass your magnificence,' I thought.

"Tender your order, Mr. Mills."

"There's one in the file your honor. The number of days granted is left blank for you to fill in, your honor."

He signed the order. I stepped back from the bench before he could find another part of my anatomy to chew on.

"He was in a jovial mood," I stage whispered to the Assistant Commonwealth's Attorney when we got outside the courtroom. She nodded understandingly. She had been an assistant public defender before going over to the Commonwealth Attorney's office. She had incurred and knew the sting of his wrath when she was a public defender. Nonetheless, I asked her if she knew Mill's first postulate of being the newest associate in a firm.

"What's that?" she asked.

"You're the low person on the scrotum pole. First to get screwed and last one to know it." Like all the other neophytes that heard the line, it got a knowing smile.

"You know what he'll do on your motion for a new trial don't you Mills?"

"Oh I fully expect him to grant it, release Sissy on her own recognizance, and apologize to her for any inconvenience that the Commonwealth might have caused her."

"You know counselor, it's that same sort of New York sarcasm that endears you to him."

"It's my No Gas Rule."

"You're what?"

"No Gas." I replied. She furrowed her brow, wanting the explanation of the mnemonic device. "No One Gives A Shit."

"Where do you get this stuff? Do you lie awake at night and think of these?"

Feigning a southern affectation I said, "No, just some outside the box dyslexic thinking. Reading English backwards teaches you that. Reading Hebrew once a week right to left preparing for your Bar Mitzvah also helped to think outside the box."

"Try all you want to, you'll never sound southern." She half-smiled and walked away.

She was right. Long ago I had given up trying to use the word 'y'all.' It just didn't sound right coming out of my Jewish New York mouth. Although I had lost most of my Yankee accent, I still didn't sound native. It sounded like I was mocking the jury instead of trying to get closer to them. At trials, I just explained my accent's origin and hoped that they felt sorry for me. Judging by my record it had worked.

I went over to the jail to tell Sissy what had happened. She had heard about the fire. I knew she would be worried that her file had been destroyed.

Chapter 5

❖❖ Everyone tries to stay out of jail. Not me. For me it was an occupational necessity. For some attorneys getting into jail was a pain in the ass. I had never sued the jailer for a civil rights violation, not that he didn't need to be, so I was on his o.k. list, which was better than his hit list. I used the side door normally reserved for officers returning prisoners because it gave me access to a better interview room and jailhouse coffee. Occasionally I took donuts for the staff, especially if I wanted to get in before 5:30 a.m. You didn't have to be from New York City to know the value of well-placed schmooze.

"Good morning counselor," came the generic intercom-voice. "Coming' to see your favorite client?"

"No, I'm here to make my weekly drop off of drugs for the inmates. You guys been doing too good a job of strip-searching the community work programmers so someone has to pick up the slack. Besides, it supplements my kid's college fund." The voice laughed, pressed the right buttons, and the first of several doors unlocked. Through a couple more and I was in.

"Coffee, counselor?"

"Donuts, officer?"

"Client, counselor?"

"Clients, coffee and donuts. What a way to start a day."

Sissy looked like she hadn't had a very good nights sleep. The orange uniform with **Prisoner** emblazoned on the back hung on her gaunt frame. The orange accented her missing two top front teeth and blackened lower teeth. She covered her mouth with her hand whenever she smiled or laughed. She didn't laugh much, even before she got arrested. She had lost weight while in jail. She only weighed one hundred pounds on the night of the shooting. I had hoped that the additional weight loss would make Walker's two hundred and fifty pounds appear bigger in the juror's minds' eyes.

"What'd the judge say?"

"He gave us five extra days to file the motion for a new trial."

"Will that make a difference?"

"Probably not."

"Then why bother? Let's go ahead and get the appeal going. I want to get the case out of that mother's hands. He won't be hearing the appeal? Will he?"

Not an uncommon question from a person unfamiliar with the process.

"No, Sissy, the Supreme Court will hear it as a matter of right." She looked puzzled. She wasn't stupid by any measure. The expression meant that she didn't understand my jargon and I needed to speak Western Kentuckian.

"You are entitled to one appeal as a matter of right. That means that by law you have a right to have your case reviewed by them. Understand?"

"I think so," she said nodding sheepishly. "What do you think we have to appeal on?"

She, like all other clients, had a right to know the issues that were going to be raised on appeal. My problem was how to put it on a level that she could understand. George Bernard Shaw was right. If you couldn't explain what you did for a living, you didn't know what you did for a living.

"First, you need to know that I won't be handling the appeal. It takes a lot of time to do an appeal and of course that means a lot of money."

"I know you didn't make any money on this case, Mr. Mills, and I 'preciate everythin' you done for me. Won't you handle it though?"

She was tugging on my sympathy organ again, not my heart. As a trial lawyer they pulled your heart out when you graduated from law school. If you were going to become a trial lawyer, they drained all your blood and replaced it with ice water. I had drastically reduced my usual fee for a murder case, not that there was a set free for any case. If I had thought that the case had a particularly interesting aspect I reduced my fee. Sometimes being right and proving it was more satisfying than the money. Putting values before money was one of those dyslexic things.

"I'm going to call someone I know in the Public Defender's Office in Frankfort. See if I can get one of their hot shots to handle the appeal. They know me from my days as an attorney in the penitentiary doing post-conviction work. I think we have one really hot issue. The other one is not too hot, but you never know what the 'magnificent seven' will grab onto."

"The who?"

"Sorry Sissy, my nickname for the seven justices on the Kentucky Supreme Court."

You always feared that the magnificent seven would see the issue but hold that you had failed to properly preserve it. Criminal practice was a procedural minefield. One missed step, one objection missed, or not followed by a motion for a mistrial, or a request for a jury admonition, and they wrote, "However this issue is not properly preserved for appeal." Their not too subtle way of saying you had screwed up.

"First, I think the judge was wrong when he ruled that Carol could not testify about what happened before the two of you left the parking lot."

Carol had been in the parking lot when Walker was shot. Carol had heard the shots. However, when she testified before the Grand Jury, she had lied about how Sissy got home. She had given Sissy a ride away from the shooting. She had told the Grand Jury that she saw Sissy walking home and did not give her a ride and was not in the parking lot when the shots were fired. How Sissy got home was not important. I had to call, or try to call Carol, and let her testify about what had happened before she heard the shots.

"Your honor, if I question Carol up to the point just before they left the parking lot then we don't get to the question of whether or not she lied about how Sissy got home and then she doesn't have to take the fifth on whether or not she lied to the Grand Jury about that insignificant fact."

"Nonetheless Mr. Mills, if the Commonwealth asks her about how your client got home then she will have to assert her fifth amendment right against self-incrimination. Then you will have called a witness who you know, or should have known, will assert her fifth amendment privilege and we both know that's prohibited."

"Judge, the Commonwealth just told Ralph Mulsum, the last witness who testified, that they would not prosecute him for perjury for lying about how Sissy got home. The Commonwealth promised him if he told the truth at trial about what he had seen and heard, and how Sissy got away from the scene, they would not pursue a perjury charge against him, and he testified that he only heard the shot. He didn't see Sissy's position relative to Walker's when the gun fired. Then I have to put Carol on and I can't put her on because 'perhaps' she lied to the Grand Jury, and then I can't put her on the stand because I can't put a witness on the stand I know will take the Fifth. And then I'm subject to sanctions by the Court."

"Look, Mr. Mills, I can't control who the Commonwealth grants immunity to and who they don't." He recognized my Hobson's choice and gloated at my dilemma.

"The Commonwealth can't grant immunity to anyone," the assistant prosecutor interjected. Simms and the judge looked at her, wondering who had given her permission to talk or even think.

"True," I replied, picking up on the softball lob pitch, "but if the prosecution promises a potential witness they aren't going to present the case to the Grand Jury, you have a get out of jail free card. The Commonwealth must keep its promises. That's the holding in <u>Workman v. Commonwealth</u>.

Your honor, if I take Carol up to the point where she left the bar then you don't get to the Fifth Amendment problem. Under the rules the Commonwealth cannot cross examine the witness on matters not raised on direct examination."

"Even when that issue goes to the witnesses credibility? I think not Mr. Mills." The old fart was not going to let Carol get on the stand. The Commonwealth did not pipe in. When the judge is arguing your case for you, shut up. Trial practice 101.

Carol had been sitting in chambers for the entire argument. She had been through the criminal process too many times before. Through this on the job training she understood her rear end was in the fire.

"Do you understand your options?" the judge said turning to Carol.

"No, your honor," she said, trying to sound believable. She knew exactly what was going on and what her options were.

"Would you like to talk to an attorney about it?"

"Yes, sir."

The judge turned to Simms, "Tim, see if you can get one of the P.D.'s on the phone to give her some advice."

He called the local P.D.'s office and explained what had happened. He handed the phone to Carol. We all left the room so Carol could hold a confidential telephone meeting. I knew the advice she was getting. Don't testify. It was a no-brainer. One, no one would tell a client to risk getting indicted for perjury, and two, the P.D. had more than they could say grace over. One more case was the last thing they needed. We returned to chambers when we saw the light on the judge's secretary's phone go out.

"Have you talked to an attorney?" the judge asked.

"Yes, sir."

"And do you wish to testify?"

"No, sir." She told the judge, looking away from Sissy and me.

"Ball's in your court Mr. Mills," he said, sitting behind his desk and glancing over at the Assistant Commonwealth Attorney and Simms. I thought I saw the beginning of a smile form in the right corner of his mouth. His judicial gambit had worked.

"Your honor, I want to take this witness's testimony by avowal."

If I was going to preserve the issue for appeal, I had to save the witness's testimony for the record. This way the Appellate Court would know what the witness would testify to and decide if the trial judge had erred.

"How do you propose to do that without getting into fifth problems?"

"Just like I would with the jury present, your honor. Take her up to the point of departure from the parking lot and stop." He gazed at the wall, running my argument through the legal analysis of his grey matter. He knew this would properly preserve the issue for appeal. Denying Sissy's right to the avowal meant an automatic reversal. Like every circuit judge, he didn't like being reversed. Like every human being, he didn't like being told he was wrong. 'I got your judicial gambit,' I thought to myself, grabbing my crotch a la Brooklyn in my mind.'

"Proceed, Mr. Mills."

"State your name, age and home address for the record please Carol."

"Can he do this, Judge? I just told you I don't want to testify." I told her I would not question her about how she and Sissy had gotten home. She eased back in the chair and answered all my questions in a calm and direct manner.

"Carol Strait, 22, 3445 Iambic Road, Mayfield, Kentucky," she said

'God!' I thought. 'The best witness and the jury won't get a chance to hear her.'

Carol related how she had been at The Valley Bar on November 25th. It was the Friday after Thanksgiving. Everyone had a long weekend. Walker had been drinking and he and Sissy had exchanged words at the pool tables. She hadn't heard the conversation but she could tell from Sissy's expression that they weren't exchanging pleasantries as they shot pool.

"What time did you leave?"

"Oh, about one thirty. Last call had been called and people were either headin' out the bar or gettin' one to go."

"Where was Sissy?"

"I don't know. I hadn't seen her in a while."

"When was the next time you saw her?"

"I heard some loud words from over the other side o' the parking lot and turned to see what was happenin.' Carol was getting nervous so I led her.

"Just relax. What did you see or hear next?"

"I heard Sissy say that Walker was not goin' to hit her. Walker said somethin' kinda like that he had had enough of her shit and that she had better keep her mouth shut. Then he pushed her."

"How hard did he push her?"

"Hard enough to knock her back a couple o' yards. She caught herself against a car before she almost fell."

"O.K. What happened next?"

"Sissy pulled somethin' from her coat pocket and held it in the air."

"Was she pointing it at Walker at that point?"

"No sir."

"What happened then?"

"Walker came at her and she said somethin' about it bein' loaded."

"What did Walker say or do next?"

"He used the "F" word, you know, like "F...you" and said that she was the only thing that was loaded."

"What happened then?"

"He kept comin' at her and then I saw him hit her and then the sound like a firecrackers goin' off. Then there was an echo. The Valley is in an old rock quarry and there is always an echo there. Even the light flashed against the walls of the quarry."

"What hand did he hit her with?"

"His left."

"How do you know that?"

"Cause Walker shoots pool left handed."

"What was said next?"

"Walker said, "damn Sissy, you shot me," like he couldn't believe it had happened. Then he started to walk back to the bar. Then everybody out in the parking lot left real quick before the law got there."

I pursed my lips trying to decide if I had any other questions. I didn't. I tendered her to the Commonwealth for cross.

"Only one question your honor."

One question? What the hell was he up to now.

"Ms. West, you lied when you told the Grand Jury that Sissy walked home, didn't you?"

Carol looked at me. I looked back, looked at the Judge and held up my hand, my fingers spread out.

"I think I want to take the fifth on that one Judge." She had understood I was not giving her high five.

The Judge nodded his understanding and ended the avowal. The Judge knew that the only witness with no dog in the fight who supported our theory of accident or self-defense was not going to be heard by the jury.

Chapter 6
Friends
❖ ❖ ❖

❖ "What's the other issue you think we got Mr. Mills," Sissy asked quietly.

"The closing argument."

"What was wrong there?"

"It's called a 'golden rule violation.' You know what the golden rule is, don't you Sissy?"

"Yea. Them that's got the gold makes the rules."

I chuckled. She could still joke about what had happened, but she wasn't joking. She had seen it all her life.

"No, Sissy, do unto others . . . ."

"Before they do it to you," she interrupted.

"Not quite," I chortled. "I know you're smarter then you let on. The prosecutor asks the jurors to put themselves in the Walker's place. That's not allowed."

"What about puttin' the jury in my place. Ain't that allowed?"

"No, same thing. I think I got that point across to them when the coroner testified that Walker outweighed you by almost a hundred and twenty-five pounds. Almost everyone who testified knew Walker's reputation for violence. That helped your case too. But that was a question of fact for the jury to decide and won't be grounds for reversal." I had never had so unresponsive a jury during voir dire. I had used some of my best lines to loosen them up. All I got in response were iceberg cold stares.

"Does anyone have a bumper sticker on their car?" No hands. Just stares.

"My favorite answer to that question was from a little lady from Clinton, Kentucky. You know what she said? " They just stared back, waiting for the punch line and probably not caring what it said.

"Don't hit me my lawyer's in jail." Every other, I mean, every other jury panel that had heard that answer at least acknowledged that it was a cute sticker with a smile or a couple of nods of their heads. This panel just stared. Not a good sign.

"If I do something that offends you do you promise to hold it against me and not Sissy? You understand that right now there are two people that can control me. One is behind me in the black robe." Easy, pause before you deliver the punch line. "The other is taking care of our two children." Not even a nod from the women on the jury who controlled their spouses. Not even a sympathetic glance from the other men similarly situated. I should have known then that it was going to be one of those days, let alone weeks.

Sissy just sat there as she realized that she wasn't going anywhere outside of jail in the future. No getting out on bond, no Christmas at home, no swimming at the lake. No Friday nights at The Valley. I saw the same expression on Sissy's face that I had seen on prisoners at the state penitentiary at Eddyville. The realization that they were powerless over their futures. Every decision made for them. All they had to do was time. It was then that I thought I saw a tear start to bubble up in the corner of Sissy's eye.

"Are you all right?"

"Yea," she half-choked. "It's just that I thought I'd be gettin' out."

"Yea, me too. The fact that we couldn't put you on the stand hurt us too."

"I didn't want to testify anyway. I would have said things that no one wanted to hear. Specially that asshole of a judge."

This was the third time that Sissy had said that. Each time I asked her what she meant. She just clammed up. No answer, just a glance at the wall or floor and a blank stare back at me like I was supposed to figure it out for myself. I had represented other clients who said that the system was involved in a conspiracy to "get them" because they knew something about so-and-so in a high position. Each time I questioned them about it further, it turned out to be a lot of paranoid suspicions supported by quadruple hearsay from confidential unreliable informants. But Sissy wouldn't talk. She wore her silence proudly. The rule in the jail and the penitentiary was that you didn't rat on a 'rappy,' a jailhouse slang reference to a co-defendant. But there was no co-defendant in this case. It was just Sissy and Walker.

The conference ended. Outside the jail I ran into Kurt. He had heard that I was in there talking to Sissy.

"Anything I can do counselor?"

"Yea, see if you can get Sissy to tell me what she's holding back."

"Probably just the usual shit that won't hold water."

He was right. Back at the office I still felt like the whole truth and nothing but the whole truth had not come out. So help me God!

Chapter 7

"Mary? Tim Mills. Yea, good to talk to you too. Listen, I've got this appeal coming your way that has a couple of hot issues."

As head of the appellate division, she heard that a lot.

"You got any fresh hot appellate attorney's up there?"

She paused. I could hear her running the list through her head.

"We just put out some new contracts. I think I've got just the person for you. Have you filed notice of appeal yet?"

"No, I'm going to do that today along with <u>In Forma Pauperis</u> Affidavit and motion. Then get you the form that asks me to spell out the issues."

"You got the new form?" she asked.

There was always a 'new' form. I wondered if all they did in Frankfort was come up with new forms to replace the old forms that worked perfectly well. When I had worked at the penitentiary they had me fill out a time sheet. Just like the Meg-a-firms in New York City where you were promoted by the number of your billable hours. The first time I saw that form I asked my supervisor why we had to fill them out since our clients weren't capable of paying us.

"So they could keep track of our time and what we were doing."

Doing? Hell, I've got four years of college, three years of law school, I just passed the bar and you want to know what I'm doing with my time? I'm practicing law you bureaucratic schmuck! My last day at the penitentiary I filled out my last time slip to reflect that for 8.5 hours I had done what the state paid me to do. Practice law! Begrudgingly they paid me for the time. I'm sure someone in accounting raised their eyebrow and commented that I just didn't fit in. They were right. That was one of the reasons I got out of there and into private practice. The other was the money. Starting pay for a Public Defender was $12,500.00 and all the shit you could take from the inmates. The lifetime P.D.'s saw me as someone who had sold out to the all mighty buck. I saw them as capable attorneys who liked the security and complacency of a state pay check. Never having enough business sense to make it in the real world. While my rise in private practice wasn't meteoric, I had gained limited notoriety.

"O.K., get me the 'new' forms and get the record ready and we'll take care of it from there." Mary concluded. I could tell she was busy and I was about to let her go. I had to make sure she knew how important this was to me before I let her go.

"Look Mary, this one is really important to me. It's personal." I had come to trust my gut reaction on things, even if I couldn't enunciate a specific reason. Earnest Hemmingway, when asked at the Algonquin Club what it took to be a good writer quipped, "You need a good crap detector." The same rule applied to my practice.

"I understand" Mary said half-consolingly, and hung up.

Chapter 8

❖❖ Was it just yesterday when I had hung up on Mary and she had assured me that she would get Sissy a good appellate attorney? No, it had been eighteen months. The kids were older, I was balder, my waist a little wider, and my life no less cluttered. Time had gone quickly for me but torturously slow for Sissy.

She had not adjusted well to life at Peewee Valley, Kentucky's max facility for female felons. The men had several prisons, ranging from maximum at Eddyville to minimum at Frankfort, but Peewee Valley was it for women.

While there, Sissy had write-ups for bad behavior, had done time in the segregation unit, and had lost some good time. She had even been threatened with loss of early parole eligibility. None of it fazed her. She did her time her way and not theirs, but now all of that was behind her. We were back to square one. Back in the county jail with a new trial date.

The magnificent seven had agreed with me on at least one point and that was all we needed. "We are of the opinion that the defendant was denied her fundamental right to due process. The trial court erred to the defendant's substantial prejudice when it excluded the testimony of Carol West. However, we do note that the trial court was relying on its interpretation of the law, as it existed at the time. We now hold that Ms. West may testify about what she saw and not be required to testify about what she may have said before the grand jury about how the defendant got home. That is a collateral issue."

While I had helped to make new law, my name was nowhere on the opinion. The appellate attorney got all the credit as she had argued the case before the Supreme Court. My only claim-to-fame was a couple of nebulous references to "trial counsel." My ego suffered no compound fracture, just a mild bruise. In the courthouse halls, other lawyers who had seen the news of the reversal in the local paper offered their congratulations. The attorneys in the Commonwealth Attorney's office were not well pleased, and that pleased me. A reverse congratulation.

"So, when do you think you will be ready to re-try this case," An assistant Commonwealth Attorney asked me, trying to change the subject, making me realize that my pyrrhic victory at the appellate level was a temporary set back for the Commonwealth.

"I don't know. The Commonwealth has more control over the docket than I do. I guess whenever the Commonwealth and the judge decide to try it, I'll have to be ready."

"Did you hear about Carol West?"

"No. I assume she's still alive. I haven't seen her name in the obits."

"Oh, she's not dead, she just seems to have fallen off the face of the earth. Word has it she packed up one night and left. No forwarding address. When we heard about the reversal we issued a subpoena for her and could not find her. And you know, if we want to find you we'll find you."

I feigned looking worried because that was the reaction she expected. I also realized that taking her testimony by avowal had been a better move than I realized. Worse came to worst I could read that testimony to the jury. It wouldn't have the same impact as if she was a live witness, but it sure beat the hell out of nothing.

"Of course you've got her avowal testimony," she chimed in, "so I guess you've got nothing to worry about."

"Yea, I almost forgot about that."

Two players working at the psychological game of getting your opponent off balance. A game I didn't like to play with any opponent, but one I found necessary to play on occasion. Get them off balance on a key point. Know that they have a way of solving the problem. Then see if they know the answer to the problem. If they didn't then they had one more thing to think about. They were distracted. Then you had the chance to catch them off guard on another point. Before long, you were on the high ground they had formerly occupied and they had no idea how you had taken them off the hill. Simms, the Commonwealth Attorney, was more adept at playing the game.

He graduated from law school top in his class. Editor of the law review, a position held only by the number one student, chief of the moot court board, and the recipient of numerous book awards for best grade in the course. He had been in private practice with a top firm, when for some unknown reason he gave up a chance to rocket to a partnership position with the firm and took a job as an Assistant Commonwealth's Attorney. As an assistant, he never lost a case and became the cop's sweetheart. He was single, not divorced, and no kids. The two were not mutually exclusive. He had all the time in the world to devote to his cases and did.

"Simms is taking over the case, you know," Anne, the assistant Commonwealth Attorney said, assuming that I was somehow privy to their morning case conferences.

"No, I didn't know that. Why the heck is he taking over the case? It's a simple no-brainer white trailer trash murder. He tried it the last time. I would think he was bored with the case by now."

"Simms didn't say. He just announced that he'd re-try it."

"I thought he had more than he could say grace over."

"You know Simms. Something gets his interest and he becomes obsessed with it."

Just what I needed. A prosecutor with a pit bull personality and a lightening quick mentality and wit. Once he got his jaws locked onto your client's throat, he didn't let go. Then he went after you. He would get you all tied up in little battles over hyper-technical evidentiary issues. You're winning small battles and then the next thing you heard was, "We find the defendant guilty."

Now I knew why the assistant Commonwealth Attorney had made the remark about Carol West. It was a set up for the killer punch that Simms was taking over the case. A nice job, but a bit premature. I now knew who my real opponent was going to be and had additional time to adjust. If Simms had waited until the pre-trial conference to show up, or better yet, waited until trial to walk in, it would have had more impact, and would have really caught me off guard. But he knew I knew all of this. There had to be something else that wasn't disclosing. That's what worried me.

"Look, I've got to get back to the office. It's been a real slice of heaven talking to you," I said sarcastically, rising from the wing-backed chair in her office and letting myself out.

I hoped I hadn't looked upset, just pre-occupied. The short trip back to the office was on automatic pilot.

Chapter 9

Gone for only an hour and there was a stack of phone messages from clients wanting immediate attention. Returning messages was like triage. Who was dying and who was salvageable. One message was truly in need of immediate attention and could wait until the afternoon.

The message from Carol West was correctly marked P-1; our shorthand system for numbering my priorities had been developed by Emily. She wrote that Carol had just called and left neither an address nor a phone number. The message Carol only said that she would call me back. Resigned to reality, I returned other phone calls. I was in the middle of one when Emily walked in and handing me a note that Carol West was on line two.

"Carol! Where the hell are you? Word on the street is that you left town without a forwarding address or anything. How would I have known where to send flowers for your birthday?"

"Mr. Mills, I couldn't stay in town. The Walker's said word on the street was that I wouldn't be around to testify if I stayed in town, so I split."

"Anyone in particular tell you that?"

"You know, just word on the street," she replied harshly.

"Look, Carol, anyone that threatens you is guilty of intimidating a witness. It's a Class D Felony."

"Great! I'm six feet under and the person that threatened me is doing one to five, assuming they even get caught. Who would give a shit if I dropped dead? Doesn't sound like a fair trade to me, Mr. Mills."

Based on what she said and the tone she said it in, I knew she'd talked to an attorney. So why had they threatened her?

25

"Is there something else you know about this case that you didn't tell me that could help Sissy?"

"Ask Sissy."

There it was again. Sissy did have some more information that she was keeping from me. Carol knew what that information was and neither one of them were going to tell me.

"Whatever the information is, Sissy won't tell me either. Is it something that will help Sissy?"

"Ask her."

"Look, Carol, I did. She won't talk. You consider yourself her friend, maybe even more. Everyone else just heard the shot and the echo and no one wants to talk about what went on in the bar before the shooting. If she goes to Peewee Valley this next time it won't be all my fault. You'll get part of the fault. Do you want that?"

She paused. I had struck a nerve. Silence is the most effective tool to getting an answer. Ask and wait for the answer. Don't help the witness, let them sit there and brood. I hoped that Carol's conscience was the jury. I waited for an answer.

"Not fair, Mills." She had noticeably dropped the respectful, 'Mister,' indicating how pissed she was.

"Life's not fair Carol. Besides, the fair only comes to the county once a year. We make certain choices in life and then have to pay the consequences for those choices."

"I didn't make no choices. I was just there. I guess I chose to be at the bar, but that don't mean that I got to tell you everything I know."

"You do if it will help your friend."

Another long pause. Her silence told me she was thinking about the dilemma.

"You know how to get to Evansville?" she asked.

"I went to college in Owensboro, I ought to."

"O.K., well I'll meet you tonight. You just say when and I'll say where and then we can talk. Just you. I don't want that Polish Afro-American PI of yours there at all."

"Carol, I can't be there tonight. It's two-thirty now. I've got appointments the rest of today and all day tomorrow. How about seven or eight o'clock tomorrow night?"

"Choices and consequences, Mills. You're not here, let it be on your head." Her street smarts made up for her sixth grade education.

"Yeah, that'll have to work. I'll come up to Evansville. Be there in about two or three hours."

"You go to the Dairy Queen on Diamond Street. It's open 24 hours. They got one of those old time stay in your car and the waitress brings you your food kind of things. I'll spot you. Then we can talk."

Emily prepared a subpoena for Carol West to appear at trial. It wouldn't be worth a damn served in Indiana, but maybe Carol, with her on the job training of the judicial process didn't know that.

Chapter 10

❖❖ The drive up the Western Kentucky Parkway is beautiful in the fall. The leaves starting to change, the reds and yellows against the constant green of the pines and cedars reminded me of up state New York. Goshen, Cheater, and Middleton. I remembered the last time my freshman year law school roommate had called me and asked me how I liked living in the boondocks of Western Kentucky, he had returned to New York and Couldn't located Paducah on a map.

"Where the hell is Paducah?" he asked.

"Halfway between Possum Trot and Monkey's Eyebrow," I answered sarcastically.

"No, really, where the hell is it?"

"It's halfway between Nashville and St. Louis."

"What's it like?"

"Well, contrary to popular your New York City belief, we wear shoes."

"Yea, but I bet they sure talk funny." He said, drawing out the 'sh' in sure with a typical New Yorker's accent.

"Come on down here and see who they think who talks funny," I said, making the 'a' in talk an 'au.'

I couldn't adequately describe the difference in the lifestyle and the attitude between the two cities and I'm sure he didn't care. He was content in the Big Apple and I was happier in the heartland.

The autumn view, and particularly the sun setting in my rearview mirror, convinced me even more that I had made the right decision. As the sun finished setting, I turned left onto the Pennyrille Parkway toward Henderson and eventually Evansville.

It had been a while since I'd been to Evansville, but I still remembered my way around. I found the Dairy Queen on Diamond and pulled in and ordered something to eat and sat and waited for Carol to show up.

"How's the food here?" Carol asked startling me.

"'Bout the same as Kentucky."

"How was the trip up?" she asked, making small talk.

"Not bad. We here to make small talk or to help Sissy?"

"If Sissy won't help herself why should I?"

"Look, Carol, I thought we already cleared that up. Otherwise, I wouldn't have made this trip. What the hell did you run from? The Walker family had shot off their mouths before the first trial that anyone who testified against their dead son would get hurt, and that didn't stop you from testifying before. What's changed?"

"If it was jus' the Walkers I wouldn't give a shit. They don't scare me. It's bigger than them." She glanced around trying to look inconspicuous, yet anxiously to make sure no one was listening.

"Why don't you get in my car and we can talk."

"No way, man. What I got to say won't take long. I came to Evansville 'cause you can't subpoena me here in Indiana with a Kentucky subpoena."

'Well,' I thought, no sense trying to bluff her into coming back to Kentucky with the subpoena I had in my right hand next to my armrest. Now I had to get her to tell me what she knew what Sissy wouldn't tell me. I reached into my jacket pocket, reaching for a cigarette, and turned on my micro-cassette recorder on simultaneously.

"You remember there was a lady that watched the first trial? The blonde, wore a dress every day, big 'store bought tits." She said.

"Yea," I said, Kurt had noticed, no glared at her, throughout the trial. I didn't pay much attention to her though. I figured she was just a spectator."

"Yea, well you figured wrong. She was at The Valley the night that Walker got shot. She had talked to Walker a lot that night and in fact, just before he got shot. No one really knew her. She wasn't a regular at the Valley. We figured she was slumin'."

"So how does she figure into the equation?"

"You notice which side of the court room she was sittin' on during the trial?"

"Look Carol, I don't have time to play twenty questions. What's your point?" I was exasperated. I had not driven all the way up here to chase down another lead generated by an unsubstantiated paranoid piece of hearsay.

"Well here's the deal," she started.

"Ms. Carol West?" came a voice from behind her.

Carol turned to see an older man in a blue sports coat, gray slacks and black wing tips approaching her.

"You dirty son-of-a-bitch Mills. You said there wouldn't be no cops. You gave me your word that you were comin' alone."

I was just as startled as she. I had no idea where the cop had come from. He along with three other Indiana State Troopers grabbed Carol. Everyone in the Dairy Queen looked over at us to see what was going on.

"I have a warrant for your arrest, Ms. West."

"Fuck you Mills! See if I tell you shit now you asshole."

"Look Carol, I have no idea what this is about. I swear to God!"

"Yea, right."

"You have the right to remain silent," he said, starting to Mirandize her.

"What's the charge officer" I interrupted.

"Who the hell are you?" He asked, obviously upset that I had broken the rhythm of his Miranda warning.

"I'm a lawyer."

"You got a license to practice in Indiana, counselor?"

"No, just Kentucky."

"Then as far as Indiana is concerned, you're just another Dairy Queen eatin' John Q. Public, counselor. Why don't you just mosey on your way and leave Ms. West to us before I arrest you for obstruction of justice."

"Look officer, I'm not trying to obstruct anything. In fact, I was trying to . . ."

"I don't give a rat's ass what you were trying to do." He interrupted, "I got a warrant faxed up here from Kentucky two hours ago for Ms. West and I was told by my chief to drop everything else and get her into custody."

"But what's the warrant for?"

"Ask the Paducah prosecutor. That shouldn't be hard for you to do now should it counselor?" I had heard the same tone from other cops that had arrested other clients before.

"All I know is that I got her and I have to hold her for sixty days to see if the Kentucky Governor wants to extradite her."

"She can waive extradition and speed up getting to Kentucky, right?" I said in a similarly obnoxious tone.

Carol was being lead off by other troopers. She turned her head acknowledging that she had heard what I had just said.

"Well, if she waives then she goes back tonight."

"I ain't waivin' shit" I heard Carol scream as one of the troopers put his hand on her head to get her into the cruiser. In a moment the door of the cruiser closed and Carol and any information she had were gone. The detective looked at me and didn't have anything else to say. He turned and started to walk away.

"Where you takin' her?"

"Jail and then arraignment in night court, counselor. I'd advise you to head back south into your own jurisdiction unless you intend to represent her and get busted for practicing law without a license in Indiana."

There was nothing I could do for her. Now two questions had to be answered. What was Carol going to tell me about the blonde and how the hell had the Commonwealth Attorney found out that I was going to meet her at the Dairy Queen in Evansville?

Chapter 11

What had just happened to Carol? Were my telephones or my office bugged? I wanted to exclude the possibility of employee disloyalty but couldn't. Keep an open mind. Don't exclude any possibility. I reached for my cell and thought about calling Kurt, but thought twice. Someone might be able to hear our conversation. I was becoming too paranoid. I called him.

"Kurt? An interesting development on my end."

"What's up counselor? It's past midnight."

"Meet me in my office in about two hours."

"Where the hell are you?"

"On the Western Kentucky Parkway."

"Why tonight."

"Look, I haven't got time to explain it all. Especially over this damn cell phone. As Warren Zevon sang,

"Send lawyers guns and money the shit has hit the fan," He interrupted.

"Anyway, be there or be square." I said, finishing the thought.

"Gotcha counselor. Be there then." While there's no autopilot on the car, I didn't remember a lot of that trip back. I think my brain went on auto and got me home. Kurt was sitting in his car outside my office. So was a blue Paducah City Police cruiser. I knew the officer in the cruiser. I had represented him in a police disciplinary proceeding and had gotten his suspension for excessive force reversed and had him reinstated with back pay. Rob O'Hara was a good cop. He did his job well. He just didn't like and didn't play the political games within the force.

"Rob, what's goin' on?"

"Bad news Tim. Your office was broken into." O'Hara said. "One of your neighbors heard someone in the office tearing stuff up. They didn't see your car outside the office and called us. Jim Bonner was the first on the scene and found Gene Malone in your office."

"Gene Malone? Mean Gene the drinkin' machine? The town drunk, in my office?" I asked. Amazing, someone who I had seen in district court on a regular basis charged with alcohol intoxication, and who I had never represented, and therefore never pissed off, was in my office.

"I'll check my schedule, but I don't think Gene had an appointment for tonight, Rob."

"I know you keep weird hours Tim, but I didn't think you kept weird hours with weird clients," Rob said sympathetically. Kurt had gotten out of his car and was standing there listening, taking it all in, wondering how, if it did, fit in with my earlier call. I was wondering the same thing.

"Do you want to prefer charges against Gene?"

"You bet your sweet ass I do." I said, venting my frustration from the evening's earlier events.

"You know the defense Tim. He'll claim he was intoxicated and he didn't remember anything. He'll just take up space in the jail. You know he won't do any hard time Tim."

"You book him and I'll go talk to him in a couple of days, Rob. Much damage to the office?" I asked, shifting gears.

"I was waiting for you. Policy dictates we don't go in until the owner is present. We might get accused of taking something."

"Yea, the last thing you need is another disciplinary hearing Rob."

Rob just smiled, acknowledging my former representation. We walked into the office. The door had been forced open. Pictures were askew on the wall. My iMac had been pushed on the floor. From the back of the office came an unmistakable odor. There in the middle of the hall was a big pile of Mean Gene's best colon contents.

"God, I had no idea that a drunk's scat stank like that, Rob."

"You get used to it in my line of work Tim. Gene has probably crapped and puked in more cruisers than any ten drunks put together. It's a rite of passage for rookies." He said, trying to make the best of a bad situation, having no idea of how bad the situation had been earlier in the evening.

"Look Rob, I'll make up a list of what is broken and what can be repaired. I'll have to do it for the insurance company anyway. I'll get a copy down to the station in the morning. You can make it a supplement to your report." Kurt had still not said a word. I looked over at him and then down at the feces on the floor.

"I do a lot of shit for you counselor, but cleaning up that shit is not in the job description," Kurt said without a smirk. Rob looked at him, for the first time wondering what Kurt was doing there. He also knew better than to ask. Kurt's presence was a client confidence and Rob knew I wouldn't tell him. I asked Rob not to put Kurt's name in his report. "Least I can do for you Tim. He was just a citizen sitting across the street. You going to be o.k.?"

"Well, I won't be going home tonight. With the door broken I'll have to sleep on the couch to protect the office. I don't think Gene found my .25 cal. I've got it pretty well hidden."

Jim Bonner, first officer on the scene, didn't find a gun on Gene when he patted him down. The only thing he found was the remains of a fifth of scotch.

"Gene's come up in the world. Drinking scotch now instead of Richard's Wild Irish Rose. I thought MD 20-20 was his beverage of choice."

"We thought he got it from your place and confiscated it as evidence."

"No, I'm a drinker, but I don't keep a bottle in the office. Keeps temptation just a little further away."

"No big deal Tim. Gene sure was drunk. He kept asking for his new drinking buddy."

"I thought he drank with Joey V?" Joey V was a local drunken midget who could out drink any two men three times his size.

"No, Joey V's in jail doing ten days for A.I. and indecent exposure" Rob Said.

"Ah, yes, Joey V. - the frigid midget with the rigid digit. He had gotten drunk and waived his weenie at some little old lady?" I asked.

Kurt tried to smother his laugh at my reference to Joey V. Rob was not as successful. He laughed, slapped me on the shoulder.

"That's the ticket Tim. When the shit hits the fan, or the floor, as the case may be, keep your sense of humor."

"Rob, you need a great sense of humor to survive in my business. I imagine it's the same way in your business too."

Rob nodded, still chuckling from the reference to Joey V. He headed out the door to his cruiser. Kurt and I heard the car door slam and headed into my office. I got some Lysol, paper towels, and held my breath as I cleaned up the worst of Gene's visit. I checked to make sure that my .25 cal. was in the right place. It was. Damn, I thought. If old Gene had taken the gun I could have charged him with first-degree burglary. As it stood now, he would be charged with second-degree burglary. Gene knew it would probably get knocked down to misdemeanor criminal trespass.

"Did you know that your office was going to be broken into while you were on the parkway counselor? Is that why you called me to meet you here? Take a course in Psychic abilities in law school?" Kurt had developed as rye and dry a sense of humor as I had been cursed with. His response to his brutal youth, also.

'I had no freakin' idea it was going on. What was going on when you got here Kurt?"

"They were just bringing Gene out of the office when I got here. I pulled up to wait for you and the cops came over to my car and started questioning me about what I was doing here. That cocksucker Rob thought I was in on the break-in and almost patted me down. You got here just in time. I was starting to get real smart with him when you pulled up."

"Well, evidently he was satisfied that you were here on legitimate business. He didn't have much to say to you when I got here," I quipped.

"I told the son of a bitch that you had called me. He didn't believe me."

"Imagine that," I scoffed, "You with a credibility problem. Look Kurt, it's been one hell of a night. I went to Evansville to talk to Carol West." Kurt sat there and listened as I told him what had happened. When I finished he just looked at me, not knowing what to say. He lit up a cigarette and exhaled hard.

"Who do you think bugged your office counselor?"

"Why do you say that Kurt?"

"Because that's the only explanation that makes sense. Emily is as loyal as a Labrador retriever. No one else other than your wife knew you were going to Evansville. Unless of course you suspect her?"

"How do you figure Gene 's new drinking buddy figures into the equation, Kurt?" The fifth of scotch doesn't fit Gene's drinking M.O. Something's going on and it stinks to high heaven."

"Even more than Gene's souvenir." Kurt quipped.

"Mama said there'd be days like this." I semi-sang, "she just never said there'd be so many in a row. It's almost three o'clock Kurt. I'm going to sack out on the couch. I'll be the night watchman. I've got my .25 cal. here. I should be safe."

"I wouldn't feel too safe with that pea shooter counselor. You want my .44 magnum for the night?" He reached inside his coat to pull it out.

"No, I'll just shoot 'em in the kneecap if they come in."

"Suit yourself. I've seen you on the firing range. At least the .44 will make more noise. I'll see you in the morning. Sleep tight."

I turned on a couple of lights and sprayed more Lysol, making it smells like someone had taken a nasty dump in a flower garden, instead of just raw scat. Sleep was little more than fitful, getting no more than ten minutes sleep at a whack.

Chapter 12

Emily got to the office ready for the daily grind. She refused to go back to her office because of its closer proximity to Gene's midnight package. I went home to shower and prepare for the grind. Emily could tell I was in no mood to go into details about the break in or any of yesterday's events. She started to do the inventory of the midnight rambler's damage. Earlier, after Kurt left, I had called 'she-who-must-be-obeyed' and had told her about the break in so she wasn't wondering where I had been all night.

Ah, hot water on my neck muscles loosened me up. I started thinking more clearly. Big Mama brought me a cup of coffee and sat it on the sink counter. She came back in after I finished my shower.

"Boy, what lousy luck you've been having lately." Consoling me, she tried to get me to open up and talk. She loved me but knew one thing about me. I always kept my own counsel. That way, I didn't have to worry about a breach of privilege. That was my rationalization. It also protected her. Another rationalization.

"If it wasn't for bad luck, I don't think I'd have any luck at all." I put the shaving cream on my face. She sat down on the toilet seat cover to listen.

"What is it with you and old rock and roll and blues songs? You always quote them. Any subliminal reason?"

"Those Oldies but Goodies," I switched gears, "What really bothers me is that Gene was drinking Scotch."

"Why? Because he didn't offer you a slug off of it?" She smiled now, trying to get me to do the same.

"No, it's just not his M.O. He's a hard-core alcoholic. If he drinks it's usually MD 20-20 or Richard's Wild Irish Rose or Bali Hi. Definitely not a single malt man."

"Maybe he just got his check," she chuckled.

"If he did, he wouldn't spend it on Dewar's. You know what I think I'll do? I think I'll go pay Gene a visit at the jail. He may not be sober yet and he may remember more about last night now than he will later when he sobers up." I said as I finished shaving around my mustache.

"Can you do that? I mean is it ethical for you to talk to him?"

"Why not? He may need a good lawyer." I said smiling out of the side of my mouth; almost nicking the labial fold running down from my nostril that was rapidly growing with age.

"You need a shirt pressed?" She asked.

"No, I don't have to be in court today. I'll just put a sweater over a shirt and no one will know."

On the drive back down to the office, the "Scotch" concept kept going through my mind. I got to the jail and buzzed the intercom. They asked me whom I was there to see. When I told them I wanted to see Gene there was a brief pause followed by an unmistakable chuckle.

"You going to represent Gene?" the voices asked."

"Yea, I don't see a conflict of interest, do you?"

"Well, he's not in a real good shape," the voice responded.

"Well, he's just graduated from misdemeanors and petty ass violations to felonies. Maybe the reality of time in Eddyville will have a calming effect on his stomach. It won't be the first time I had to talk to someone with a hangover. It probably won't be the last either."

"Bring in the chump," the voice said. I didn't know which of us the voice was referring to.

I ushered myself into the attorney's meeting room, went over to the TV and turned up the volume. Not because I couldn't hear the TV but because of the effect I hoped it would have on Gene. When Gene walked in he looked like death riding a horse eating a sandwich. He entered wiping away the vomit from the corner of his massive facial labial fold.

"Morning, Gene. Remember me?"

"Yea, you a lawyer. But you ain't with the public defender's office."

"No Gene, I'm the son of a bitch whose office you broke into last night," I said looking him right in the eyes. He looked at me like I was telling him a lie. He kept looking, trying to remember what had happened. Then he got that look. The look that told me it was all coming back to him.

"Oh, you mean the trip with the Terminex guy," he said laughing.

"What fucking Terminex guy Gene?" I said sternly, my voice pissed off and the look in my eyes even more pissed off.

"Guy said he worked for Terminex and he needed some help. Said if I helped him he'd buy me some of da good shit. We got da good shit and I finished about most of it when he said it was time to go to work. Said he'd buy me 'nother bottle if we finished work real fast."

"Yea, right Gene. Did the guy have a Terminex company shirt on?"

"Yeah, man," he continued. "I never seen him before, but he had on the uniform to match his talk. We got to da place and he knocked. There was no answer. He fumbled for a second. I think he was looking for a key while he stood in front of the door blocking my view. He told me to stay outside, so I did. He went in. I stayed outside and took a couple of hits off da bottle. He went in and come right out. Asked me if I had to piss and told me where da bat'room was. I went in. Nice office man. I never had nothin' dat good. It pissed me off dat someone had nice shit like dat so I thought I'd fuck it up a little. You know, knock some shit on da floor,"

"That's when you took the dump?"

He smiled, showing his ethanol-extracted teeth. "Nice touch huh?" He smiled, more of last night starting to come back.

"I finished and decided to get da hell out. Terminex had locked the door behind him and I couldn't figure out how to get out, so I pulled real hard on the handle. It come off in my hand. Next thing I know, da fuckin' cops is crawlin' every fuckin' where."

"You see anything in the guy's hand when he walked out Gene?"

"Nah, he just patted his shirt and asked me if I had taken a piss. He didn't ask about the scat. Man dat sure was good whiskey."

"Well, I hope to hell you enjoyed it. It's going to be your last for a long time."

"What you mean man? I'll be outta here in a couple of hours, back on the street in time for my morning hit."

"Not today Gene. Last night you graduated to felony status. You might as well resign yourself to the fact that you're in here for a long time this time."

"No fuckin' way man? I don't get outta here in a couple of hours, I'll be in the DT's man."

"Not a pretty thought is it Gene?"

"I want my lawyer man. Dis' is a bunch a bullshit," he said, the thought of the DT's starting to sink in.

"I think I'll go see the judge now Gene. I think I can get him to set your bond at about ten thousand dollars cash." Emphasizing the last word.

"No way man," he said pleadingly, looking me in the eyes.

"Yes. Way man." I replied unsympathetically. I started to get up and leave. Gene just sat there with his hands covering his ears, looking at the glare off the linoleum floor.

"Man that fuckin' TV is givin' me a headache."

"No, the whiskey's giving you the headache. The fact that you ain't goin' to get no hit for the next couple o' months or years is what's making your stomach hurt," I said in my best street vernacular, hoping to drive the point home.

I headed for the door. "Man, you can't do this to me."

"I can and I damn well will." I was resolute and he knew it.

"Man what da fuck ya want from me?"

"Tell me who the fuck it was that went in my office," I screamed. The deputy jailer in the glass control booth looked into the room, surprised at my overbearing tone. I looked back letting her know that everything was all right. She went back to staring at the control panel.

"Man, not so God damn loud. I'm in the same room." I walked over and lowered the volume on the TV. Beginning the good cop mode. I sat back down in the chair, pulling it just a little bit closer to him. Not too close though. If he lost his stomach contents one more time I didn't want to be down range.

"Who the hell was it Gene?"

"Man, I told ya. I never seen the fucker before."

"All right Gene, I believe you. What did he look like?"

"Like a big bottle o' good shit," he said, trying to remember. "He was 'bout as big as me. He had on a nice fresh bug company uniform. Not jeans, and not a suit. Definitely not the sort of go to church clothes like the Seventh Day Adventists wear. Ya know man."

I sat there saying nothing. Just listening. Silence – a great tool for stimulating conversation.

"Man my fuckin' head is killin' me. Oh yeah, speakin' of heads, he had one of the ugliest rugs I ever seen."

"You help me, I'll help you Gene."

"Ok, man, let me think." A novel notion for Gene. One I was sure he hadn't pursued in quite some time.

"You're doing good Gene. What else?"

"Nothin' man. I think I'm gonna be sick."

"Hold on Gene. I'll get the jailer." Too late. Evidently the process of thinking and remembering was too much for his vaso-vego system. He dry heaved. He rolled to the floor, holding his stomach, hoping that something would come up. Nothing came up so I got up and looked over at the control booth. I could see that the lady in the booth was on her walkie-talkie calling another deputy jailer. In a moment two deputy jailers walked into the room.

"Easy Gene," one of them said.

"Yea, it won't be long 'til you get your morning' hit. " The other one chimed in, hoping to get him to settle down.

"Not likely," I said.

The two of them looked bolt up-right at me. The thought of having to dry Gene out did not please them. I had the power to get him out and they knew it. I could make their next ninety-six hours a lot easier if I just let the old drunk out so he could get his next drink.

"He's all yours boys," I said.

"Thanks, Mills. Just what we needed," one deputy grunted.

I headed out of the jail and over to the courthouse to the county attorney's office to check on Gene's arraignment. Terminex man. Nice touch, stupid, but a nice touch of irony. So, there had been a bug in my office. Whoever the hell it was, wanted to get it out before I had a chance to realize that I had it in my office and sweep for it. I knew that stuff like this went on in big cities like New York, Chicago and LA, but not in a small town like this. What the hell kind of information did I have that someone wanted to bug my office? The couple of personal injury cases I had didn't involve any products liability against GM or Ford or any of the big shots that might want to do it. Sissy's case had already been tried once. The Commonwealth had all the testimony. There weren't going to be any new witnesses. Why? And perhaps more importantly, who? Or maybe who and why. Instinctively, I dyslexically reversed the order of analysis.

The county attorney's office was just opening up when I got there. The gauntlets of secretaries were just settling into their morning coffee and their exchange of Mary Kay trivia. I walked past them to the county attorney's lead secretary's desk.

"Good morning Mr. Mills," she chirped. "Heard you had a little excitement last night."

"Yeah. Buddy in?" I asked, referring to her boss. Buddy was a sharp contrast to the Commonwealth Attorney. Buddy had worked as an assistant for most of his life until his predecessor retired. Now it was his turn to be the boss and deal out the trash cases to his assistants and keeps the high publicity cases for himself.

She picked up her phone and buzzed Buddy. "Go right in." I ambled down the corridor, knocked, and let myself in.

"Morning counselor," Buddy said, leaning back in his chair, nestling his chin in his right hand. "Here to see about the bond on your midnight visitor?"

"Yea, Buddy. I think I've got more than a passing interest in it."

"We're going to recommend time served."

"You're what?" I said, immediately from cool to ballistic. He could see the rage in my face.

"We can't get Gene for burglary. The most we can make is criminal trespass first degree. Class A Misdemeanor."

"Hell you say. The bum went in my office and took a dump."

"Ain't no crime in that counselor. More like Gene exercising his First Amendment right to free speech. Letting us know what he thought of criminal defense lawyers in general." He said, trying to get yet another rise out of me. He had succeeded.

"Look Buddy, he entered a building with the intent to commit a crime therein. Taking a dump on my carpet is criminal mischief. That's the crime committed therein. Right?"

"Correct counselor. Look at it from a social engineering point of view. Isn't that what you're always pitching to me and juries?" He smiled, recognizing that he had turned one of my own arguments on me. "We keep him in jail for twelve months. Dry him out. He gets out. He gets drunk again. What have we accomplished besides feeding him for twelve months?"

"I can see the headlines now Buddy. County Attorney releases burglar after one day in jail." Now I had struck a nerve. Nothing bothered Buddy more than the paper criticizing him. Public ridicule. A politician's worst nightmare. He tried to hold back a wince but failed

"Let them talk. Election is not for a couple of years. It will blow over."

I could tell I was getting nowhere fast. "Thanks Buddy. If I can ever do anything for you, be sure not to call me."

"Look, Tim, if Gene were your client you'd be saying the same thing to me." He said trying to console me.

"Yea, but I'm not the lawyer. I'm the victim. Someone bugged my office. I've got to find out who it was."

"What do you mean bugged?" He sat up. Now, I had his attention.

"Can you think of any reason that Gene would break into my office? What did he want to do, some late night legal research? And what about the guy that was with him?"

"What guy?" he asked. "I didn't hear anything about another guy. All I heard from the jail this morning was that Gene had broken into your office."

"Look, I just got through talking to Gene at the jail. Hold him in there for a couple of days. If I don't have anything from him in seventy-two hours, you can cut him loose. O.K.?"

"Yea, sure Tim." He was more conciliatory now. "I didn't know about the other guy and the bug. You got any proof of the bug?"

"Terminex." I said, starting to rise from my chair. He looked at me curiously and didn't respond.

"Sorry, Tim. I didn't know the full story. Call me if you want me to get the city detectives over there to help you."

"I don't know where this thing goes Buddy. Do me a favor. Let me handle this. Not a word to anybody. I mean anybody! The wife, the staff, the Commonwealth Attorney."

"Sure, Tim. Whatever you say." He rose from his chair. I felt badly about my earlier unkind remark and accepted his peace offering handshake. I walked out of his office and contemplated going back to the jail to tell Gene that he was not getting out today. I thought again and realized it would be better if he heard it from the judge. That way he could sit in his cell and wonder just how much I could do for him, based on what I had just done to him. Yeah, let him cogitate and ruminate on that for a little bit.

At arraignment the judge told Gene that the County Attorney requested a ten thousand dollar cash bond. The judge set it at a thousand dollars cash, not knowing or caring the reason why the county had requested it be set so high. A thousand, ten thousand. It didn't matter. Gene couldn't make a hundred dollar bond.

Chapter 13

Kurt was at the office when I got back. I filled him in on what Buddy had said and more fully about what had happened with Carol West in Evansville and how I thought it tied into the break in.

"Regardless of how they figured out where West was, what do you think the warrant out of Kentucky was for? A sealed indictment for perjury? Use it as leverage?" Kurt asked.

"No, not even the Commonwealth Attorney's office would be brazen enough to screw with the Supreme Court's ruling. Maybe it's for something else, like accessory after the fact. That makes more sense."

I gazed and hypothecated, mumbling to myself "Assistant Commonwealth Attorney tells Carol West's attorney that if her memory has faded the Commonwealth will drop the charges since she, on her own, can't remember how Sissy got home. Maybe she can't even remember exactly what she heard or saw. People commit perjury all the time in divorce cases. Sometimes even in criminal cases, and the Commonwealth never bothers to indict them. What was so special about West?"

"She knows more than she is telling?"

"And I don't think it's so much what she knows. I think it's what she knows but still hasn't figured out the impact of what she knows about whom. Whatever it is, it's scaring the daylights out of someone."

"Who?"

"Hell, if I knew that I'd have all the answers. All I know is that I think that the babe that sat through the trial has something to do with it."

"How do you know that?"

"Because that's all that West got out of her mouth last night before she got busted. If I can just get to her and let her know that I had absolutely nothing to do with getting her busted, she might tell me."

"Still nothing out of Sissy?" He asked.

"Tighter than a well digger's ass," I said. "Look, I'm going back to the jail to talk to Sissy and tell her what happened to her "good buddy" West. Maybe that will loosen her up."

"You want me to go to Evansville and see if I can talk to West?" Kurt asked, hoping that I would say 'no.'

"No, you'd probably get there after visiting hours. Besides, there's no guarantee that she would even talk to you. Besides, trial on Sissy's case is just a week away. I have more important things for you to do."

"Like what? Serve a bunch of last minute subpoenas?"

"No, like trying to find out who the babe in the court room was. You're the one that thought she was so good looking. I'm surprised you didn't get her phone number. Introduce yourself; tell her how important you are to the case, work your seat with the big boys into a phone number or better, a date. Maybe even use those beguiling Polish-Afro-American looks into a late date,"

"If you'll recall counselor, I was busy guarding your ass in case the bailiff screwed up and aimed wrong."

"And don't think Big Mama didn't appreciate it. She could be sittin' pretty right now on the insurance proceeds alone. Look, I'm going to jail. You get the subpoenas from Emily and call me tonight at home and let me know how many you got served. I'll let you know how things went at the jail then. O.K.?"

"Whatever you say Kimosabi. Me serve subpoenas. Find witness. You send up smoke signal if need help." He grinned as he rose to go back into Emily's office.

Entering the jail always has a sobering effect on me. It makes me realize that perhaps there was someone up there looking after me. I don't recall, nor do I care to recall, how many times I entered it and thought, 'There but for the grace of God go I." All the stupid stunts I had pulled as a youth and college student, and had not gotten caught. All done to get acceptance among my friends who were non-plussed with my lackluster academic accomplishments because of my dyslexia. Then too, there was some of my trips home from the war room with one too many Dewar's under my belt to be safe on the road. Yep, no doubt about it, someone up there liked me.

"Yo! Little lawyer, I really need to talk to you man," came a scream from the drunk tank. I turned to see Mean Gene the drinking machine much more sober than I had seen him that morning.

"Sorry Gene," I said. "I can't talk to you. You and I are on opposite sides on this one buddy." Being the good cop could still help.

"Give me a break man. I really need a hit of some shit. I'm really sorry for what they say I did to your office man." He said, still not acknowledging or knowing what exactly he had done intentionally.

"Yea, that's it Gene, start to build your defense," I said unsympathetically. I turned to the deputy jailer and told him I wanted to see Sissy and started to walk toward the interview room.

"I think I can tell you more about the Terminex man," he said hoping to get my attention.

"No way, Gene. You weren't much help this morning and I doubt if you'll be much more help now."

"If you don't talk to me soon I'll be spilling my guts to the snakes and frogs that will be crawling all over me in a little while."

I looked back at the deputy jailer who nodded his agreement with Gene's last statement. He too knew all too well that in a little while Gene would be climbing the walls.

"Let me think about it Gene. I've got someone else to see and after I see her I may talk to you, o.k."

All I heard was "Give me a break man," as I shut the door to the interview room behind me. A few minutes later Sissy was sitting in the room with me. She was sullen over the thought of the impending re-trial.

"I found Carol West," I said, waiting to see her reaction.

"Big deal, she won't be much help. Look, is it too late to cop a plea in this case?"

"She said to ask you about the blonde in the courtroom. What do you know about her?"

"Ask Carol when she gets here for trial. You got her subpoenaed, don't you?"

"I was going to when the Indiana State Police busted her. I think there was a sealed indictment for perjury out for her."

Sissy didn't say anything. She shook her head and muttered her version of the golden rule again.

"Look, damn it? I can't defend you if you won't help me let alone help your fucking-self, Sissy." She looked startled. I had a foul mouth around the office and friends; I tried to keep my mouth more professional when talking to clients, colleagues and the court. The change in tone captured her attention. I capitalized on it.

"You know who the fuck she is, or what the hell she was doing at the Valley the night Walker was killed, right?"

"Look man, Peewee Valley really ain't all that bad. At least when I finish my time I'll be alive."

"If the people who you are afraid of are as powerful as you seem to think they are then they can have you taken care of in Peewee. Then you won't be getting out of there alive either."

"I made it fifteen months last time didn't I?"

"And that's no guarantee that you'll make it out the next time."

"Man, get me a plea to time served and I walk out of here."

"All right Sissy, I'll go see Simms, but if he doesn't do a 'time served deal' you're on your own."

"What do you mean by that man? You can't quit on me now."

"I can't? Just watch me." Lack of client cooperation is always grounds to get out. I stood up and pushed the intercom button and told them to "Fucking come get her." The interview was over. She sat in the cold metal chair staring at the floor, not knowing what to say.

"What about the money my people paid you?"

"Long gone Sissy. I've earned that and then some. If I billed them for all the time I spent on this case they'd be working for the next ten years to pay my fee."

She sat there digesting that thought. "All right. You talk to Simms. If he won't do 'time served' come back here and we'll go from there.

Finally! I had gotten through to her that this was not some game. All I had to do was interject a "fuck you" or two.

"I'll go see Simms right now Sissy. Then I'll come back and talk to you." She half-smiled, characteristically covering her mouth, and nodding.

Outside in the main jail area I could hear Gene. The deputy jailers were standing around drinking coffee. As the gate opened to let me into the main area, they turned in unison and looked at me, pouting and wondering if I was in the least bit sympathetic to their impending plight – Gene's detoxification.

"All right," I said, "if it will make you guys happy I'll talk to Mean Gene the drinking machine. But he's going to have to sign a Miranda waiver first. You got any handy. It's not a document I carry around."

"Shit, Tim. We got more damn state issued forms around here than anyone needs. Bill, go get this fine lawyer a Miranda waiver." I walked back to the interview room and sat waiting for Gene.

Chapter 14

I had not smelled the odor that emanated from Gene since I had roamed New York City's Bowery in the mid-sixties. It was the unmistakable combination of urine, vomit, and perspired alcohol. All combined in a fragrant un-bathed bouquet. They could have at least cleaned Gene up a little before I met with him. A deputy jailer's joke no doubt. Either that or they were trying to give me a finer appreciation for what they dealt with on a daily basis. I wasn't amused.

"O.K., Gene, let's make this quick," I said trying to hold my breath between sentences.

"I gotta get outta here, and I mean pronto," he rasped. "You got a cigarette?"

I handed him a cigarette and lit one up myself hoping the smoke would cover up his odor. All that did was add another layer to the existing aroma.

"You said you had some more information for me about the Terminex man."

"First things first, little lawyer. I give you the information and you agree to reduce the charges, or at least the bond so I can get out. O.K.?"

"You're not in the strongest bargaining position Gene. I walk out of here right now and you stay. How's that?"

"Man I need a hit," he said exhaling heavily. I gasped for a breath.

"Look Gene, I need to know who you went into my office with last night. You help me and I'll see what I can do for you. The more you help me. The more I'll help you. That's the best promise you're going to get. Also, before we talk any more I want you to sign this Miranda warning."

"Man, you ain't no cop. I don't have to sign that."

"You're right Gene, you don't," I said as I started to get up and walk toward the intercom to buzz it to get out of there.

"Wait man, don't do that. Here, give me a pen and I'll sign the freakin' thing. There," he said, signing an "X", his mark. "Happy?"

"You done real good Gene," I said, putting on my best Western Kentucky accent. "Who was the Terminex man?"

"I never seen him before. He came in the Red Cat Bar down on Third Street and started buying everybody drinks. Now I remember he did have on one of those Terminex company shirts and pants. Shoes didn't match the uniform though. Looked like cop's shoes. After about an hour he came up to me and asked me if I wanted to go help him with a job he said he had to do. I asked him what kind of work. He said some kind of pest control, bug control. I told him I used to crawl under houses doin' insulation work. He said he knew that 'cause the others in the bar had told him that. I asked him what the pay was and he said he'd buy me a bottle of good stuff and give me fifty bucks. He also said it would only take a couple of minutes. I was pretty blasted at that point and figured I could use the stuff and the bucks to finish my buzz off for the night and still have leftovers in the morning to help me start my day off right."

"Again, what did he look like, Gene? What did his face look like?" still trying to hold my breath and light another cigarette.

"He was about your age. He had a beard and a mustache. He was heavier than me, but not fat. That freakin' toupee. I think he combed it with that bug spray shit."

"Did he have a tie Gene?"

"Nah."

"What color was his toupee?"

Gene laughed. "Man he must a-been like Mr. Clean under that rug. It was that bad a rug. He made you look like you had a full head of hair." It was Gene's way of putting me down for going bald. Gene may have been a drunk but he had a full head of hair. He never missed an opportunity to tell a bald guy that he had that up on him.

"What else do you remember Gene?"

"Man, that's it. I remember him tellin' me to use the screw driver to open the door before he used the key."

"You didn't think that was odd Gene?"

"Hell, I was toast. Once we got in he told me to wait there while he did his pest control thing. He walked in and a half a second later he was back outside. I said I had to take a wicked piss. The shit was an after thought. He said to go use the bathroom in the office, that you wouldn't mind. That's when I said I had to take a shit too. He said go ahead and do it in the middle of the office. We both laughed, so I dropped trousers and crapped. The next thing I knew, I could not get out and there was cops everywhere."

"Gene, a long time ago I had a friend install a burglar alarm in my place. I had the signal go directly to the Paducah Police.

"Well, little lawyer, why did that guy need me along?"

"He probably hoped that the cops would see it as a drunk causing mischief and leave it alone. Evidently the cops and everyone else bought into that. They haven't talked to you Gene, have they?

"No man."

"All right Gene, you've sort of kept your part of the bargain. One more thing, here's my card. You call me if you see this toupee-wearing clown again at the Red Cat or anywhere. I don't care what time of day or night. You call me. There are a couple bottles of good stuff in it for you and maybe even a dismissal of these charges if you give me the right man. Bullshit me, and things will, and I mean will, get worse. One last thing. This conversation never took place. You didn't roll over on the Terminex man. That keeps you safe, and keeps me looking stupid. Deal?"

"Yeah, got it. What are you going to tell the County Attorney?"

"I have no problem knocking your bond down, but the charges stay. Call it leverage Gene. That way you get out. One more thing. I find out that you've seen Mr. Terminex and haven't called me; I'll get a warrant for obstruction of justice so fast that your head will spin like you been drinking grain for a week and just stopped. We clear on that, Gene?"

"Yes sir," realizing that I still held the trump card, but that he was getting out.

I got up, buzzed the intercom, and was out. I called Buddy from the deputy jailer's area so they could hear me, tell Buddy I had no problem reducing Gene's bond but they were to hold the burglary over his head. The deputy jailers sighed. Gene was getting out before he detoxed au natural. More booze, less detox.

"Bless you counselor," one deputy jailer said as I left. "In a coupl'a more hours we'd a had a Mean Screamin' Gene on our hands. Not a pretty sight."

Now, whoever had planted the bug would think that I thought that Gene acted alone. Who would believe otherwise from the delusional town drunk anyway?

Chapter 15

Simms was in his office holding a staff meeting. I waited outside his office reading the victim impact brochure that they kept around the office. It explained the judicial system to victims. A detective from the sheriff's office came in. Detective Olst was well built, and well connected and like fifty per cent of the other detectives, clean shaven from the top of his head to his neck. If he was clean-shaven below that I did not want to know. Nor was I inclined to ask a cop groupie from the local cop-bar.

"How's it been going?" I asked.

"O.K. Just got off a three-week vacation. Back to the old grind. You know how it is counselor. We bust 'em; you defend 'em; they go to jail. They get out, we bust 'em again, and you defend 'em again. They go to jail again. You think you might get a few acquitted to speed up the process? It's a vicious circle and the only one who makes any money is you.

Olst had been the first officer on the scene at the The Valley Bar when Walker was shot. He was always bragging about his conviction rate. If he charged a defendant, they got convicted. If he got a search warrant, the judge always found probable cause to get the warrant. His warrants were never tossed at a suppression hearing.

The staff meeting broke up. The receptionist came out and granted Olst the first audience with Simms. Olst smirked, like the kid who cut in line in the high school cafeteria. He went into Simms office.

"I'll only be a minute counselor," he said as he closed the door behind him.

"I'm sorry," the receptionist said. "I thought he was here first."

"No problem. What I've got to talk about will take a while. If Olst keeps his word he shouldn't be here long. I don't think he has the intellectual ability to carry on a protracted conversation."

She smiled, went about her filing and waited for Olst to finish his audience. She turned from her filing. "Sorry to hear about what happened with Gene at your office."

"Yea," I said looking up. "As if I didn't have other things to do with my time."

Before she could retort, Olst exited Simms's office and was out of the anteroom door just as I had predicted. She called Simms on the intercom, smiled, and pointed to his door indicating that I had been granted an audience with the "man with the dirty knees" as I called him. "The head man."

"Tim, how the heck are you? How are the kids? I saw the article in the newspaper about your triumph over dyslexia. An interesting article, yes sir. I sure learned a lot more about the disorder. Tell me, does it affect you at trial?"

The paper had learned from a colleague, who I had confided in – but would never confide in again, about my battle with my learning disability. Back when I was a kid, educators were moving from the nomenclature, SLD – specific learning disability, to dyslexia. Educators were even starting to figure out dyscalculia, the learning disability associated with numbers. A disorder my daughter had begun to show evidence of.

"Spell it like it sounds." I could hear my father saying in the back of my head. "It sounds like I am spelling it," I thought to myself.

"You're not listening to the sounds of the letters." A book flew across the room and hit me in the head.

"Oh, yeah, I could hear the sound of the letter a lot better now, Dad."

I never got an apology from the old man when he and mom figured out it was not my fault. My brain was just wired differently. Evidently whacking it with books and objects did not re-wire it.

I settled into the chair across from Simms's. "Fine, fine. The last time I saw the kids they were fine. You know all too well how this business takes up your time and away from friends and family."

I didn't say anything else about the local paper's coverage. The writer had done a three-part series on dyslexia. He started with kids who had the problem and had followed it up with a piece on their teachers. The final part was on people, like myself, who had succeeded, or appeared to have succeeded, in overcoming the learning disorder. Evidently the conversation I thought was confidential with a colleague had come back to haunt me. As a trial attorney the less your opponent knew about you the better off you were. Knowing about personal habits, drinking too much, womanizing which took up valuable time, or a reading disability gave them an edge up. His reading disability, takes him longer to read cases. Less time for detail. But then again, Simms knew I was an early riser too. More time to read and catch up. What Simms and others did not know was that when God gave you lemons, he helped you make lemonade. God had blessed me with a better than average memory. My memory had made it possible for me to get through my Bar Mitzvah. Hell, I memorized the entire service – Torah, Haft-torah and the entire fourteen pages of the afternoon Musaf Service. Whew! Once I learned something it was mine. Like the rules of evidence. I knew all twenty-three exceptions to the hearsay rule, and could quote them almost verbatim. I knew Rule 404 (b) on the admissibility of prior bad acts better than 98 percent of the attorneys in the Commonwealth. I had argued and won the leading case on rule 404 (b) before the Magnificent Seven. Most judges respected my mastery of the rules. All but one, and he was presiding over Sissy's case. Again.

What I hadn't disclosed in the article was that I had recently been tested for ADD. My suspicions were confirmed. I was ADD-RT. Attention deficit disorder-retained type. The prevailing theory behind ADD was that as a child passed through puberty they outgrew the disorder. The testing had confirmed my theory. I had overcome my dyslexia utilizing my ADD early morning wake up calls to get work done while others slept.

"So, Simms, do you think there is any hope of us settling Sissy's case?" Getting right to the purpose of my visit.

"What did you have in mind Tim?"

"Oh, I don't know, knock it down to manslaughter second and call it even at time served. West is testifying this time."

"Don't be too sure of West. The deal might work if I didn't have the family to consider and if I didn't care about what the paper might say. How about your client does ten years on manslaughter first. That's as low as I can go."

"What was West indicted on?"

"Can't say, sealed indictment."

"Come on Simms, you and I both know that West is going to testify this time. You may have her indicted, but I can get her here under the Interstate Compact. If anything, she will create a reasonable doubt about whether or not it was intentional, accidental or self-defense."

"Save the closing argument for the jury Tim. If we try this case I'm going for murder again."

"Did you see that blonde sitting on your side of the courtroom during the first trial?" I asked, trying to catch him off base.

"I saw her. Why do you ask? He said, starting to shift around in his chair, trying not to look concerned.

"I was wondering why she had an interest in the case?"

"How the hell am I supposed to know?" He said. I could tell he was starting to get agitated. Had I hit a nerve? Simms rarely, if ever, cursed or raised his voice. When he did, I knew that I had struck a nerve. I decided to keep pushing.

"She didn't look like the usual spectator, a little too high class to be that. Do you know her?" I asked pursuing the point further.

"Hell, Tim. There are all sorts of people that show up to watch a trial. I have no idea who she was. What's all this got to do with your client taking a deal?"

I still wanted to explore the blonde. Ever since Kurt had pointed her out, I thought back to the trial. She had followed Simms out of the courtroom every time there was a recess. Maybe Kurt was right. There was a connection between Simms and the blonde. Maybe I would try a bluff on him, and see how it played.

"I thought I heard someone say that they saw you at the Valley bar with her."

"If I was with half the babes that people say that they saw me with, I don't think I would have time to try cases. Who said they saw me with her anyway?"

Now he was trying to get to my source. "I don't remember. It was a while back. There was a blonde at the bar the night that the shooting took place and West said that she saw the same blonde talking to Walker before he was killed. I just thought it might be her and she might have some information that related to the shooting. Any thoughts on that, Simms."

"You've had open discovery into our file. We don't have any statements from anyone meeting her description."

Generally, there was nothing particular about a bill of particulars. The actual document was filed to make the Commonwealth put flesh on the bare bones of the indictment. It failed because the Commonwealth had 'open file' discovery. Everything in their file was open to discovery. That really didn't help either because invariably a cop showed up the day before trial with a document that he had failed to file with the Commonwealth's Attorney. This judge let it into evidence citing my lack of due diligence. Open file my butt.

"Open discovery is only as good as what the police and the other people put into your file. If the officer doesn't think that the information is pertinent then I don't get that information." For a long time the courts had ruled that defense lawyers were not allowed to do a fishing expedition through the cop's files for fear that we would discover their 'reliable confidential informants'.

"Are you impugning the reputation of the officers, Tim? You know that could be actionable." Simms said trying to shift the conversation.

"Moi? Impugn an officer's reputation? No, I just think that they have a different definition of what's relevant. That's all. I don't like being at their mercy when it comes to deciding what I do and don't need. That's all." He had shifted the conversation away from the blonde and I wanted to pursue it further.

"Would you enter an agreed order that I can look through the investigator's file to see if any of the other people at the bar saw the blonde there that night?"

"No way Tim. It sets a dangerous precedent. If you think we're withholding information take it to the judge. Is your client interested in the offer?"

I eased back in my chair. He knew the judge would never let me into those files unless he agreed. Still, there was something about his nervousness that set my visceral crap detector quivering.

"No, I'm only authorized to take a 'time served' deal. Looks like we won't be able to agree. I appreciate your time Simms. If you change your mind call me. If Sissy changes her mind I'll call you."

We rose and shook each other's hand. When he grabbed mine he looked past me, trying to look through me and figure out what I was thinking. I gave him a blank stare, hopefully creating the impression that not only was there nothing there, but there had never been anything there. I don't think he bought it. He was either too smart or knew me too well to believe that there was nothing lurking in my mind.

I left his office and went back to jail to tell Sissy the news. Normally it disappointed me when I couldn't settle a case. It meant hard preparation for trial. This time though, I felt exhilarated.

Chapter 16

❖ Sissy was not pleased, but she didn't cry. She stared off into space trying to figure out how all of this was going to go down and how she would end up when it was all over. Unfortunately, she didn't have the cognitive skills to think all the way through a problem, and its logical consequences and legal conclusion. If she had, she wouldn't be where she was now.

"What happens now?" she asked, hoping I would help her figure it all out.

"We go to trial. You tell me all about the blonde like you said you would just before I left."

"Do I have to?"

"No, you can keep your mouth shut and get the same result as last time. Happy?"

"Can't you get that information from West?" She asked, hoping I would not ask any further. Enough of her jerking me around. I had other things to do than sit around and hold her hand. I stood up, lit a cigarette and started to leave.

"Where you goin'?"

"Enough is enough Sissy. I've been to Evansville. I've had my office bugged and almost torched to the ground. All because of you and some blonde you say knows something about this case. If I were charging you by the hour you couldn't have afforded me past the preliminary hearing, never mind for the re-trial. All you want to do is play a game. Well I'm tired of it. You just bought yourself a free ticket to the public defender's office. You play your games with them. I've got bigger fish to fry." I pushed the intercom button.

"Y'all done in there Mr. Mills?" came a voice over the speaker.

"No, he ain't done," Sissy shouted.

"Are you all right Mr. Mills?" the voice asked.

"Yea, I'm O.K. Give me a couple more minutes." I returned to the chair behind the desk.

"O.K. Sissy lets have it. Cut the bullshit." She looked down at the floor. This time she knew this was her last chance.

"The blonde was at the Valley the night that Walker got shot. She had been there a couple of times before. No one really knew her. She would come in all dressed up turnin' all the guys' heads. It pissed off women. She shot a pretty good game of pool so I knew she had been around. She played pool with Walker a couple of times. The night that Walker got shot she had gone outside with Walker a couple of times. Carol and I been watchin' her and figured that she had gone out and burned one with him. Maybe even done a line. Pretty Babes always got it free. She come back in and looked at us the same way we looked at her. You remember they found a couple of joints in Walker's coat pocket when the coroner took his clothes into evidence."

"Yea, no big deal. So Walker liked to get high. Why would you be concerned about that?"

" Well, he always carried at least two ounces with him on the weekends. After the blonde and Walker come back in, Walker come over to Carol and me and started to brag. He said he now had protection now. Carol West asked him what he meant and he said that she was the sugar baby to some big shot in the courthouse."

"So?" I said. It wouldn't be the first time that someone in the courthouse was keeping a babe on the side. Besides, the blonde could have been bullshitting him." Simms wasn't married so he didn't have a wife to hide her from. The judges were too old for her. The Circuit and County Court Clerks were happily married, or as happily as anyone could ever be in the institution of marriage.

"He said that she wanted to buy some pot, a little snow, and some X and vitamin V for her and her sugar daddy to do the next time they got together. He said she had to be real cool about it because if anyone found out who she was doing it for and with that it would blow the lid off the courthouse."

"Did Walker say who the sugar daddy was?"

"No, he just smiled and said that he knew who she or he was and that what he knew was sure to give him some protection."

"Did she hang around the bar after they came back in?"

"Yeah. Walker didn't have no snow on him but I think he knew someone in there who did. He had the X the V and the pot. She wanted to only go through Walker. He walked around the bar after he talked to us and talked to a couple of other guys who usually hold. Carol paid more attention to who he was talking to than I did before he went back outside with the blonde."

"I know the rest from there," I told her, having heard it all at the first trial. "Walker came back in and got into it with you. The two of you were told to leave, or take it outside. You and he exchange words. He comes at you and pushes you. You think he is going to shoot you, so you pull the .25 hoping it will scare him off. I know the rest."

"No you don't know the rest. You just heard what you heard at trial."

"I know," stopping her interruption, "what West is going to say? She'll testify that Walker was coming at you and that you were justified in thinking that he was going to hurt you. Given his past history of hitting people, regardless of gender. She gave you a ride home instead of letting you walk home like she testified at the grand jury."

"That ain't all we saw and heard."

"What else did West see and hear?"

"When we heard the echo we turned around. The blonde was standing next to a Lincoln. She was leaning on the roof holding what looked like a pistol. I ran to Carol's car thinking she was going to shoot me. As we pulled out we saw the blonde go up to Walker and take the drugs and the gun that Walker had in his left pocket. At that point Walker had already fallen down. As we pulled out she just pointed her right hand at us like people do when they fake having a pistol in their hand. Her thumb dropped down like a hammer on the gun. We got the message.

"I had aimed to miss Walker, scare the shit out of him. I may be a lot of things, but I ain't a bad shot. I'm a country girl. I didn't shoot him. She did. Unlucky for me she carried a woman's favorite weapon too, a .25."

"Was there anyone else in the parking lot Sissy?"

"Other than West and her an me? No one that I could tell, but there were a lot of cars. Hell, Mr. Mills, it was cold in November. No one was standing outside. Least ways no one I saw. I didn't have time to turn around and take a photo. Me and Carol got the hell out of there. On the way, I tell Carol how I had to say it was self-defense. I'm tryin' to think of an alibi. No one was goin' to believe what we saw. He did have a pistol on him; only she took it off of him. Still, every one knew he packed. So we went with self-defense and the 'he pushed me hard story', best we could do at the time. Carol says, 'what was I doin' giving you a ride. Hell, that throws her in the ditch too. Don't it?"

"And did Carol see the flash too?" I ask.

"Yeah and she saw the flash of the gun against the what is it you call it, grotto, is that what you call it, wall? But she didn't tell the grand jury that. We real, I mean real good friends. She didn't tell the grand jury about the blonde getting the gun or pointing her finger gun at us either. West understands the golden rule real good."

"So why tell me this now. Why didn't you or West tell me this before?"

"Because Walker said the blonde was connected to the court house. Who was going to believe me? Some blonde that no one knows did it? What's that got to do with me killin' Walker? West and me figured she showed up at trial to let us know that she was connected. Let us know she was untouchable. Slam it in our face. We talk and realize we're in deep shit. Do we want to get in deeper or just take what is going to happen anyway? Cops investigate and she is nowhere even mentioned in any reports. You think she's not connected?"

"And you and West bought that?"

"The golden rule Mr. Mills. I ain't never had nothin' and knew that people that did have somethin' got what they wanted. Ain't that how it always works?"

I battled the illiteracy about dyslexia to prove that I could go into a business based on reading and writing, but misconceptions of the poor, that the judicial system only worked for the rich was a tougher battle. People, injured by doctors who had no business doing surgery. The Po' folks afraid to sue the doctor because they were afraid that they couldn't get medical treatment in the future. Po' people screwed by insurance adjusters who told them that no lawyer in town would take their auto accident case because the person that hit them had money. It was a paradigm that the poor bought into, and passed down from generation to generation. It angered me to no end. It was one of the reasons I took the cases like Sissy's.

"Sissy, if I thought that was the way it worked I wouldn't do what I do. Now that we have this new evidence to go on, I'll get Kurt on this. I've got to get the paper work ready to get West back down here."

"But you said she won't waive extradition, so she'll be up in Indiana when we need her at trial won't she?"

"They can't do that to you Sissy. Besides, there's never been a law passed that a good lawyer can't find their way around. Even if she doesn't waive extradition, they have to make her available for trial. There's a statute that we can use to get her here for trial and still keep you off the witness stand. Maybe I would put Sissy on the stand this time. No sense in worrying Sissy with that thought now.

We had to keep Sissy off the stand at the first trial because she had a past record, not judicial, but by reputation and character, for violence. A reputation almost as bad as Walkers. If we put her on the stand Simms would eat Sissy alive. Just before I was going to put Sissy on the stand, Kurt had learned all about Sissy's record for violence in Casey County where she had lived for a couple of years. "Bar brawls between bitches," is how Kurt characterized them. Based on my concern over Sissy not being able to withstand cross examination, and the newly discovered evidence, I decided not to let her testify. That was why West's testimony was so critical. She had seen Walker as the aggressor. Now I knew she had also seen another shooter, or at worst another possible shooter. Her testimony was even more critical.

Now that I knew more about what the blonde had done, I could talk to West and convince her to testify about all that she had really seen and heard.

I got up and pushed the intercom button. The voice came over the box.

"You done in there, Mr. Mills?"

"Yeah, stick a fork in me. I'm done."

"You sure this time?"

"No doubt about it. Right Sissy?"

"Yeah we're done," she added, looking down at the floor then looking up at me, covering her smile.

Chapter 17

❖ If Simms thought that he could keep West out of the picture by having her arrested he had only had half a thought. Simms was methodical, well thought-out, even diabolically on the ethical edge, but never half-witted. Nothing that he could possibly control was left to chance. If he could not control it and guarantee a victory he bailed out and an assistant got the case. The only thing Simms hated more than failure was the failure to recognize that failure was impending. That was why I could not figure out why Simms had West indicted and arrested. He knew that I knew that West, regardless of her extradition status, could be brought back to Kentucky to testify and then returned to Indiana to await extradition back to Kentucky on her own substantive charges. Admittedly a ludicrous process, but sometimes due process, at its worst, was absurd depending on your perspective

Who got Carol indicted and arrested at this point was not significant. It was a sealed indictment and no one could or would talk about it. But Simms knew about it because he ran the office and he knew everything that happened in his office, or at least he was supposed to. I just needed West back here for trial. Emily worked on the pleadings, I would file in the morning to get West back for trial. Kurt had just returned from delivering the subpoenas to the other witnesses that we needed.

"If you thought that the witnesses went south at the first trial, just wait and see what their memories are like two years later counselor."

"Come off it Kurt, It can't be all that bad, can it?" I asked.

"No, its worse. A lot of these people have forgotten because they want to forget. Others forget because they have been going to The Valley bar every night since the shooting. Their brains have followed the old buffalo theory."

"O.K. I'll bite, what is the old buffalo theory"

"Coyotes follow the buffalo heard. The oldest buffalos are picked off because they are the slowest and least able to keep up with the herd. Same way with big time drinkers. The slowest brain cells are the first ones picked off by the alcohol."

Generally witnesses fell into two different categories. The first simply don't want to be bothered with missing work to come and testify. The second figured what good would it do. Therefore, they didn't want to remember. Now Kurt had given me a third category. Kurt pulled out a cigarette and lit it.

"Do you think that the blonde will be there for this trial?" Exhaling a huge plume of smoke.

"You still got the hots for that blonde don't you Kurt." I was not going to tell him what I knew."

"I got the hots for anything that good looking counselor"

"Regardless of species."

"Low blow counselor. If I could though, I wouldn't mind serving her. With a subpoena, of course."

"Have you heard anything on the grapevine about how the Walkers are taking the reversal and the new trial?"

"You mean like have they calmed down and are they willing to talk to Simms to get a better deal cut? No, no word on the street."

Kurt had connections on the street I did not want to know about. He was my ethical shield, so to speak. He went and saw and said and did things that I could not do. But he knew the line. He just knew where to stretch it. The children of Holocaust survivors were by-and-large driven to succeed. When his mom had come to the United States from a displaced persons camp she was already pregnant. A gift of life she carried with her from the death camp. She had married a well-built well-educated Black man because she had fallen in live with him. Plain and simple. Race did not matter to her. She had seen people killed because of their race, their religion, for no reason. Life was all that mattered- a lesson more of us needed to learn. She was truly a woman ahead of her time. As a result, so was Kurt. He grew up in Louisville on the south side. He attended Catholic school because it afforded a better education, not because it followed his mother's religious preference. Religious preference had landed her in Auschwitz. Now it was not going to stand in the way of what she wanted for her son. Kurt was a black belt several times over in Tai Kwon Do because that is what you needed to be in Louisville growing up with a white mother and a black father. Arian features and a black father, Kurt had acquired his mother's sense of irony.

"Ironic Kurt, well then I guess you will get your wish granted by the litigation fairy."

"I didn't know you were gay counselor." Kurt interrupted

"I'm not Kurt. You get to serve the blonde with a subpoena."

"Then you know her name?" Kurt asked, his interest piqued.

"No, I thought that was your job. You get her name, Emily will type it on a subpoena, and you serve it. We go to trial, I ask the right questions, and Sissy gets acquitted. You do the legwork, I look like a genius. Isn't that how it worked?"

"Spare me your sarcasm counselor, I know how the game is played. Anything else you need while I'm out trying to find the blonde?"

"No, Kurt. You find her and we'll agree that you have earned your day's pay." Emily came in with the papers for West. I was now distracted with the final draft of the motion to return West to Kentucky. Kurt looked at Emily, recognized that I was in a different zone, put out his cigarette and quietly vanished out the door.

"What happened to Kurt?"

"He left right after I brought you the final draft of the motion. That is the final draft isn't it?" Emily asked hoping she would get home by 5:00.

"It's on the iMac isn't it?"

"Yes it is Tim, are there any major revisions?"

"No Emily, just some small stylistic changes. You go ahead and pack up. Close Sissy's file on your iMac and I'll make the changes from here. Have a good night."

The changes to the motion were made in a couple of minutes. Now, how to change the defense without letting Simms know what I knew.

Chapter 18

I wish I could have been a fly on the wall of someone's office when they heard that West was coming back to testify. A little known provision of the law allowed a Kentucky judge to order an out of state judge to issue a subpoena to an out of state witness requiring that witness to appear back in Kentucky. It was a statute generally used only by the prosecution. I saw no sense in not making it work for the defense. Sauce for the goose, sauce for the gander. After all, wasn't that how we got the reversal in the first place, by making the rules apply equally for both sides. Take that gambit your honor. If our motion was in order, which it was, he had to grant out request.

"An interesting argument Mr. Mills. I should order a Vandenberg County judge to grant you an Indiana subpoena ordering Ms. West to appear here in court to testify for you and then allow her to return to Indiana to then be extradited back to Kentucky if Kentucky still wants to extradite her?" He asked. I've only seen this done by the prosecution.

"That's right your honor. The way I read the law, Ms. West would be ordered to appear here to testify and in consideration for her honoring the subpoena, the court is required, under the statute, to grant her immunity from service of process for any outstanding warrants and even form service of process in civil suits while she is here in Kentucky under this order. The statute does not say anything about this being the prosecutions exclusive tool. Does it Mr. Simms?" I said, turning to him

"What does the Commonwealth have to say about all of this Mr. Simms?"

"Judge", Simms said, in that slow deliberate southern accent, letting me know he was still thinking because he did not like the answer that had formulated in his mind. "I'd like to do a little more research on it, but I think Mr. Mills is right. We've already had this case reversed once because the Commonwealth took advantage of the rules, and I would hate to see it happen again. Can I have a day or so to respond?"

Under normal circumstances, that judge would have given Sam until doomsday to do anything he wanted but time was short and this judge never tolerated a last minute continuance, even at the Commonwealth's request.

"I can't give you too long Mr. Simms. The trial is set to begin this coming Monday and I hate to waste a jury or the court room time."

"I understand judge. Why don't you grant Mr. Mills' motion and if I come up with any last minute research I can fax it over to Mr. Mills and you can give us a hearing on it."

"Suit you, Mr. Mills?" The robed one asked.

"You know me judge, anything to move the process along."

'Yea sure,' I could hear the judge thinking. 'Anything to get me reversed you illiterate Kike-carpetbagger. You may have won the last round but the game was just starting. I will be the rule maker. Rule number one is: Thou shall have no other rule makers before me. Rule number two— when in doubt see rule number one.' He rose from his chair and all others rose in respect.

The stare from the bench was a little confusing. He wanted to rule against the motion. He hoped that Simms would give him any reason to deny the motion and Simms had failed him. He had no other choice but to grant my motion. But what did he care if West came back. It was just another trial to him. He had won re-election two years ago. Did his personal animosity for me blind his judgment so much? No, maybe it was the shit eatin' smirk on my face from having won the motion that he didn't like. Whatever the reason, I had bigger fish to fry. I had to get Kurt up to Evansville to tell West she was on her way down here for trial. I probably needed to talk to West myself to explain to her what had happened, what Sissy had revealed and how she was going to come back to Kentucky without having to face the perjury charges. She had not told the grand jury about the blonde because no one knew to ask her. Not telling the grand jury everything was not perjury. She would still want to know how she got indicted and who testified before the grand jury to get her indicted. Two questions I still could not answer. Kurt would have to deliver the news. None of the details that I had just become aware of. Just the news she was on her way back. Kurt was a trusted member of the team. Emily was even more trusted. Big Mama the most trusted. Early in my career, I had learned a valuable lesson. If you want to keep a secret, tell no one. What Sissy had told me would remain with me and only me until I needed it. What I had figured out about Sissy's real relationship with West would be my secret too. One I would reveal only if required to by necessity.

Courtesy is an effective scalpel in the hands of the right surgeon. While I was not a master in the operating room I was a master at getting information out of the Circuit Court Clerk by the courteous application of innocuous questions. If you were nice to the ladies in the clerk's office they would help you get anything you needed. Make one mad at you and you had the entire civil service system's wrath against you. 'Keep the Clerks happy!' Should have read the sign outside their door, a variation on Dante's admonition to all about to enter the gates of hell. I asked for West's file from the clerk in charge of the criminal division.

"That's a sealed indictment Mr. Mills."

"Not any more, she was served with it a couple of days ago in Indiana. No big secret any more."

"Let me check on that Mr. Mills."

'You do that you bureaucratic so-and-so and see if maybe for once you're wrong and I'm right.' I thought. 'Now now. Temper temper; remember the sign outside that gate. Within a couple of minutes she had found the file and learned that the indictment had been served. Therefore, she thought it was no longer under seal. She was wrong; service of the indictment did not unseal it. She would tell no one for fear of losing her job. If she got mad at me for having her get me the information no other clerk could figure out why she was mad at me and ignore her wrath. Reluctantly she handed me the file. I turned to the indictment and saw two things. Only one witness had testified before the grand jury and Simms was not the prosecutor who had presented the case.

Chapter 19

It really should have come as no surprise that Olst had testified before the grand jury against West. As far as he knew, she might muddy the waters of his investigation about The Valley shooting, as she had done before, but she didn't have any information that would completely blow his case away. Or did she, and did he know it? I had never known Olst to go this far in a case. West was not indicted on perjury. That would have been in contravention of the Magnificent Seven's remand. Aiding and abetting after the fact was reaching, but not in contravention of the Magnificent Seven's remand order. Olst, the cop's cop, could not have figured out that this was the way to go. I had to ask him who had told him to go to the grand jury directly to get this indictment, but I couldn't because I had come by the information surreptitiously.

Armed with this new information I called Kurt. He drove me to Evansville so I could work on the way up. Little did he know that he was not going to be involved in the interview with Carol. It would piss him off if he knew he was just a glorified chauffer. He would have to get over it. We stopped at the Vandenberg County courthouse and got the local judge to sign the necessary papers. Simms had come up with no reason to stop us. We walked to the jail to see Carol. It was then that I told Kurt to wait outside. I was wrong. He was not pissed. Boy, was he pissed! It was an insult. An indication I did not trust him. Screw me for making him my chauffer. As expected, she was not in a very receptive mood. She was still under the impression that I was the reason that she was there. "If you think for one minute that I'm going to talk to you, you're out of your mind."

"Good to see you too Carol." I said. "I've come to take you back to Kentucky."

"You can't do that Mills. I haven't waived extradition and I'm not about to do it now. By the time I get through with that process Sissy's trial will be over and then maybe they will drop the perjury charges against me. So what do you think of that Mills?"

"Sounds like you've been talking to some jail house lawyers."

"Yeah, and they're a damn sight better than you, you no good son of a bitch. Bringin' the cops down on me like that."

"Now wait a minute Carol. I had nothing to do with that and you should have already figured that out. What good do you do Sissy in an Indiana jail?" I could see her mind working through that concept.

"I don't know. Maybe you were bought off. Hell, I don't know. None of this shit makes any sense to me since the night I got arrested."

"I was serious when I told you that I had come to take you back to Kentucky. I have the papers here signed by the judge that allows a Kentucky cop to come and get you and bring you down for trial and then he has to take you back to this wonderful mansion in Evansville to await extradition."

"That don't make sense. How come Kentucky doesn't just keep me while I'm down there?"

"You want a six hour course in extradition law or you want the short version? Here is a copy of the Vandenberg judge's order. Read it. If you have any questions I'll be happy to answer them." I sat back and let her read the papers at her own pace. I could tell when she got to the part about not being subject to service of process for either criminal or civil suit. She just smiled and looked up at me. She knew how cool this was. At that point, I think she realized that I hadn't been bought off and that I really was on Sissy's side.

"You mean that I get to go testify for Sissy and then come back here to Indiana and while I'm in Kentucky they can't touch me or make me stay there and face the sealed charges?"

"That's what it says, doesn't it?"

"That's really cool. I mean it's like being superman and even kryptonite can't hurt you. Cooooool!" She exclaimed with a half grin. There was a pause and then the realization hit her.

"That still ain't no guarantee about nothin'. That blonde is still going to be there and you and me don't want to know who she's connected to Mills. If I go back to Kentucky, I ain't talking! Sissy will just have to do her time. What I said at the 'vowel' is all I'm sayin'."

"It's 'avowal' and I've talked to Sissy and she has told me all she knows about the blonde. I know that Walker said that the blonde had a sugar daddy at the courthouse and that she thought that she was bullet proof, which made Walker bullet proof because Walker had sold her some coke, X, V and pot."

"That was Walker's problem. He didn't understand the difference between immunity and bullet proof." She smirked and I couldn't help but smile with her.

"Tell me what Sissy told you about the blonde lady."

"I'll tell you about what I figured out about you and Sissy."

"What?"

"That you are more than friends."

"How you figure?"

"Who else would put their ass in a sling for someone who had just shot someone. Who else would lie before the grand jury thinking that they were helping? Who else would give them a ride away from a murder scene?"

"A dummy would. That's who would."

"No Carol, a lover."

West had stuck to Sissy like glue through out the night at The Valley. She said so in her description of what went on in The Valley that night.

"Every time Sissy, looked at what Walker was doing, you said, you were with Sissy. But you were out in the parking lot before she got there. You were waiting in the car for her. No other way, you could have seen and heard it all. Right? The two of you were leaving anyway."

She sat there looking at me.

"You saw the blonde out there after Walker got shot. If you said what you really saw you were a dead bitch. But you didn't have Walker's immunity. Did you? All you had was what you and Sissy saw after the second flash and the echo. The echo and the flash were not from Sissy's gun." Now she knew, I knew, what only she and Sissy knew.

Now she stared at the floor.

"Only one missing piece." I said.

"What's that, Mr. Wise-ass lawyer?"

"What's the connection between you, Walker and the blonde that would make you sacrifice Sissy?"

"First, who says you got the first part right? Second, who says you got the last question right?"

My visceral crap detector was going off wildly. I must be right! She never stopped me while I was drawing my conclusions. Anyone else would have been shouting denials, shaking their head, or telling me that I was full of shit as I unraveled the theory.

I could have told her the other details of what Sissy had told me but I had to know if their two stories were consistent. If not for the sake of justice, a commodity missing from the trail, then for my own sanity. I had not come this far and waited this long to be denied the truth. The only way to be sure I had found it was to be sure that she and Sissy corroborated each other, and I had to have the motive right.

"Mr. Mills, the way I see it I can take the stand and tell you everything just like I did a couple of years ago in the judge's office. Still think you need me as a witness?" She asked.

"No doubt about it." I smirked back. She now knew that Sissy had told me about the blonde and the second shot. She did not know how I had connected her to the blonde and Walker and setting Sissy up.

"One other thing Carol, Simms or a Kentucky cop, or any cop for that matter, comes to talk to you at jail, you lawyer up, and don't tell him squat. Understand?"

"Suits me fine."

"Remember, if you need a good lawyer when you get back to the Commonwealth and all this is over, and you got the money, give me a call."

"When hell freezes over." She quipped.

"About the same time I'd agree to represent you too, Carol." Burning bridges was never a good idea but sometimes my anger got ahead of my mind and I just had to let it have its own way. The deputy jailer let me out.

"Are you crazy for talking to her alone? Suppose she denies what she just told you. You have no witness, i.e. me, to say what she really said. You really are not all that bright are you? Or did you have a back up tape player like I taught you?" Kurt asked.

"Nope, no tape, just us talking. Remember what King Lear said Kurt?" He looked at me not knowing what would come out of my mouth next. "There is method to my madness."

"You sure that wasn't Hamlet?" Kurt smiled.

Kurt still looked puzzled. I didn't explain my strategy to him at this point. Not because I didn't trust him, but because I still had only one witness to what had seen really happened out at The Valley that night and what the blonde knew. West would have to testify, Sissy could not. The testimony out of Sissy's mouth alone made it look like another 'grassy knoll' testimony. Long ago I had taken Mark Twain's adage to heart. "It was better for me to keep my mouth shut and let all around you think you are a fool than to open your mouth and remove all doubt."

Chapter 20

At best, weekend trial preparation is exasperating. At worst frustrating, boring and aggravating. This is especially true in a case you've tried a couple of years ago. You have to get re-psyched. Reviewing witnesses' testimony from the last trial, re-writing questions, try to decipher old hieroglyphic notes from the last trial. But reward came with the adrenaline rush when the first juror was called and you knew that all the work you had been doing was about to pay off. Or at least you hoped it paid off. You had to work the case backwards. Figure out what instructions the court was going to give. Then prepare witnesses questions and testimony to fit those instructions. Then work on your opening and finally voir dire. To set the jury up so they were not fair, but fairer to your side.

Then there were the unexpected breaks that you occasionally got, if the muse of litigation shined on you. The famous fifties trial attorney, Louis Niser, "It never ceased to amaze him how inspiration always came to him at three in the morning in the law library." I had found, after my short but brutal years of practice, that it often took three to four hours of office work to produce one hour of usable courtroom material.

This was not necessarily true of jury selection. Jury selection reminded me of the fable about the bird, the cow and the cat.

A little bird was flying south for the winter. It was so cold the bird froze and fell to the ground in a large field. While it was lying there, a cow came along and dropped some dung on it. As the frozen bird lied there in the pile of dung, it came to realize how warm it was. The dung was actually thawing him out! He lay there all warm and happy, and soon began to sing for joy. A passing cat heard the bird singing and came to investigate. Following the sound, the cat discovered the bird under the pile of cow dung and promptly dug him out and ate him.

The morals of this story are:

1. Not everyone who shits on you is your enemy.
2. Not everyone who gets you out of shit is your friend
3. And finally, when you are in deep shit, keep your mouth shut.

The lessons learned by the little bird apply to jury selection too.

1. Not every juror who treats you like shit is your enemy.
2. Not every juror who answers questions and tries to treat you like a friendly juror is a friend. Sometimes they are trying to get on your panel with their own agenda; and finally
3. Don't waste good questions on bad jurors. If a juror has made up their mind, shut your mouth and move on.

It's the ability to know when to apply which rule that determines your degree of expertise as a trial lawyer.

While picking a jury is not a science, it is definitely an art. Some lawyers hire jury consultants to help them pick jurors. Look at a juror's body language; look at the demographics, economics and education level. All information available on the questionnaires jurors fill out when they get picked for jury duty. Hell, I was sociology major in College. I could do that. I always figured if you hire a jury consultant to help you pick the jury you might as well let the consultant try your case.

I had gotten so good at jury selection that more often than not I could tell you who the jury foreman was going to be. Besides, I always had Emily and Kurt with me to watch the jurors' body language. Who the jurors looked at when they got into the jury box, their reaction when the judge read the indictment. Voir dire took Simms and me about the first half of the first day of trial. Simms went first. He was so smooth.

Chapter 21

❖ Before Simms began his voir dire we had agreed that 'The Rule' would apply. 'The rule' was the rule on exclusion of witnesses. This way one witness could not hear another witnesses' testimony. A real make sense rule.

"Now I want to make sure I have each of your names right." Methodically, he went down the list of names. He knew he had written each down correctly. This was his opportunity to look each juror in the eyes, make that personal connection with them.

"I have some standard questions for you and if you have an answer that embarrasses you let us know by raising your hand and we can come up to the bench and talk to the judge privately. OK?"

'How nice of him' the jurors must have thought to themselves, 'he is so respectful of our privacy.' The jurors thought. Normally the judge asked these questions or made these comments, but this judge let Simms do this. He knew it helped Simms. Anything to help the Commonwealth was his mantra.

"Now this case involves a murder. Does sitting on a murder case cause you a problem?" Simms asked closed-ended questions to get he jury to his side. Closed ended questions did not require jurors to give a long explanation about their opinions. He was not interested in their opinions. This was his opportunity to shape their opinions to conform to his. Pre-form them, if you will.

"If the facts and the law warranted it, could you send someone to the penitentiary? Could you send them there for as long as life?"

"Objection your honor."

"Basis Mr. Mills?" He said glancing over his Bed Franklin glasses, showing his obvious disdain for my interruption.

"The law requires that they be able to consider the range of punishment, not just the maximum." I wanted the jury to understand I was more than a potted plant in the courtroom.

"I'll re-phrase the question your honor." Simms replied.

"Out of fairness, could you consider the range of punishment?"

'Oh what a nice gentleman. He is so accommodating to his opponent.' They must have thought.

That didn't turn out like I wanted it to. I looked like a jerk and he looks like a saint. I need to re-think my use of objections one day.

"This case involves a shooting out at The Valley Bar. Is everyone familiar with the location?"

Those that weren't familiar were noted. Those that were familiar were double noted. Maybe they had been there? Maybe they had been drunk there? I sure as hell wouldn't ask those questions in follow up. Who wants to admit in public they have been to such and such a place and gotten shit-faced, especially, in a conservative setting like jury selection? Just the fact that they were familiar with the bar was all we were going to get.

Simms' staff of, two secretaries, two Assistant Commonwealth Attorney's and Olst were also taking notes about the juror's answers. It was not cat and mouse. It was more then personal, dog eat dog, or high stakes gambling - prison versus freedom. Who needed to go to the Gambling boat in Metropolis, Illinois, when you played for these stakes?

I think every trial lawyer in my generation, with the exception of me, read Harper Lee's 'To kill a Mockingbird'. I saw the movie. Much easier for a dyslexic. The pursuit of 'Tzadek', Hebrew for justice, was compelling. The magnificence of this courtroom was compelling. If I ever became a trial lawyer, Aticus Finch's courtroom was the one I wanted to try cases in. Not the courtrooms of my youth.

I grew up in a small town in New Jersey, just across the Hudson River from Manhattan. The municipal courtroom was over a fire station. It was neither majestic nor compelling. The cases decided there were not significant, at least not to a pre-teen onlooker. I sat there, every Wednesday night in the summer and watched the lawyers peacock strut around, acting important. Occasionally looking out into the public, to make sure the public was looking at them. Small courtroom, inflated egos, small minds.

Courtroom "A" in the McCracken County Courthouse was everything that Harper Lee could have described. The Oak paneling, the oil paintings of all the judges that had ever presided there from 1874 forward, all made you aware of the depth of your profession. The plaque dedicated to Alben Barkley, President Truman's Vice- President, hung on the front of the judge's bench. The witness's raised chair, in close proximity to the judge's left making the witness acutely aware of their oath. Counsel's tables, large twelve by five solid oak with black curtains allowed you lots of room to spread out your case and visually impress the jury with your preparation. Dark Blue suit, wingtip shoes, white shirt, conservative tie also added to the perception of a well-qualified lawyer. Sometimes perception was better than reality, especially when picking a jury

Chapter 22

Trials are a fun challenge. Not for the client, but for the attorneys. It is a chess match played out on a twelve by four board called the jury box. Square forty-eight and you had the probabilities for a verdict. How each juror read a particular witness in combination with his or her peers' read impacted the verdict.

If a trial is fun, voir dire is hilarious. The art of smoke and mirrors at trial. A craft, if well honed and well practiced, obtained desired result.

"Does anyone have a bumper sticker on their car?" I had used it in the first trial and did not give it up.

A collective stare indicating, "Huh.

You can tell a lot about someone based on a bumper sticker. Is there a "W"? Is there an NRA? Is there a sticker left over from a recent election? Is there an 'I 'heart' my pet' on their bumper? It's the subtle messages that they sent that I looked for. Something about thinking outside the box and being dyslexic and Jewish went together well. Seeing the world backwards and upside down and understanding it from a different angle. Funny ha-ha or funny – weird? Funny incite, maybe? Like my father's Russian mother said about chicken soup when I had a cold, "It couldn't hurt."

In Voir Dire you had to defuse all of the Commonwealth's bombs.

"You will hear during this case that the events happened at a bar. How many people think that it is 'wrong to drink'?" Four blue haired Baptist women's hands flew up.

"If the evidence showed that Sissy and Walker had been drinking could you still be fair and impartial to her?" The same four blue hairs shook their heads, 'No'. It doesn't matter what the other evidence is, you could not keep an open mind, could you?"

"No sir." One responded, the others nodded their heads in agreement.

"And theses are beliefs you have held for a long time and would not give up, would you?" Another collective nod followed.

"You honor, we move to strike these ladies for cause."

The old bastard looked over his Ben Franklin's and stared right at them. "Ladies, if I instruct you that you are to judge this case on its facts and not on your beliefs, can you do that? Can you decide this case upon the facts and the law?"

Who in God's creation was going to tell the Lord high executioner, the judge that they were not going to do what they were told to do?

Each nodded their acquiescence.

"Motion overruled, Mr. Mills."

Great, there went four of my six free strikes. And the judge knew it too. Next I had to explore for cops in the family as distant as first cousin. But you had to explore for political conservatism as well. Then you had to bring them over to your side. Doing it drove Simms nuts.

"Mrs. Tyler, I don't mean to pick on you, but I checked the voter registration and you are a registered democrat, it's matter of public record. Mrs. Tyler look should have killed me on the spot. Not an unexpected reaction. I did not tell her that I had done the same with the other jurors. Simms made a note to have his staff do the same for the next trial.

"Now that does not mean that you voted for a democrat in the last election. In fact, I guarantee I will not ask you how you voted. That is absolutely none of my business and I would defend to my death, and right now you might want me dead, she held back a nod, you're right to keep that a secret. But from a political standpoint do you see yourself as a conservative or a centrist democrat? The reason I ask is because Western Kentuckians have historically had no problem crossing political lines. We, showing I identified with her and them, voted for Ronald Regan yet put a democrat into Congress at the same time. Go figure?"

"The real reason I ask is because if you had a near and dear relative on this jury this the sort of question you would want me to ask a potential juror? Think of it, if one of your children or a niece of nephew were on trial isn't this the sort of information you would want me to seek from his or her potential jurors?

She nodded approvingly. Now get the rest of the panel on your side.

"You all, deliberately avoiding 'Y'all' would want me to do the same for a relative of yours, wouldn't you? You see, I'm not trying to be intrusive into your lives; I'm just doing my job. As odd as that may seem to you"

They all nodded approvingly now. 'There you go mate', turn them your way. Now they were seeing things from Sissy's standpoint. Simms didn't see that one coming. Now, the fait a complete. Now that they were not pissed off at me for invading their political privacy I threw the hook.

"How many rate yourselves as conservative?"

Count the hands, Emily Kurt, Sissy. Mark them on their jury panel list.

"How many liberals?"

Emily, Kurt and Sissy marking furiously.

"How many center of the aisle? Emily, Kurt and Sissy's marks made furiously. Simms' team trying to keep up with us.

"How many are Jeffersonian Democrats?" This elicited a look of mass confusion.

"Thomas Jefferson was a social liberal and a fiscal conservative. How many fall into that category?"

Sissy, Kurt and Emily marked their scorecards with "J's". These were the jurors I really wanted. All of the other political questions were just red hearings.

The trick was getting the jurors talking to you. Ask them open-ended questions, instead of the "Who agrees with this or that law." Hell they all believed in the law. Instead, ask them how they felt about your client not testifying in a self-defense case. You had to approach that one carefully. Their puzzled look was understandable and anticipated.

Chapter 23

"How will we know what she was thinking if we don't hear it from her?"

Good point Mr., ugh, Go-ball is it?

"Yep, just like it sounds."

I had thought long and hard about how to approach this and Goball gave me my entrée to the rest of the jurors. How many of you agree with Mr. Goball? There is nothing wrong with his point of view. In fact I think he is right."

"Then you explain it to us Mr. Mills."

There was a universal chuckle. Even the judge and Simms joined in the fun. Some lawyers say to never ask a question that you don't already know the answer to. That's a stupid rule. Things came up all the time at trial that you don't anticipate. My credo, 'Never ask a question that you cannot handle the answer to.' So it was with Mr. Goball.

"Lets try it this way Mr. Goball. I have a friend that likes to hunt. Me, I have no business owning a gun. Never learned to use them in New York City where I grew up. I'm lucky to know which is the business end." A small chuckle came from some of the pistol packing jurors

"My friend likes to carry his shot gun in his pickup in a gun rack behind him in the rear glass of his truck. Think he ought to be arrested for that Mr. Goball?" He shook his head, wondering where I was going with this line of questioning. Instinctively he knew to be wary of lawyers.

I happen to be Jewish. Some of you are Baptists, some Methodists, some Episcopalians, Catholics, some Lutherans, and some, other religions. Did I miss any? How about the police come and arrest me for being Jewish. You all agree they can do that don't you?" Heads shook 'No.' in unison.

"How about I stand on a soap box in front of the court house and speak about the evils of our county and city government. Now there is something I ought to get arrested for. Agreed? Come on folks raise your hand if you think I ought to be arrested for that." No hands.

I had them all, not just Goball, listening and answering now. Now Simms and the judge were wondering where I was going. Simms didn't object because he thought he was getting as much information as I was. He wasn't. I was not running a law school. If he made a mistake it was my job to capitalize on it, not educate him.

"How about this, a colonel from the U.S. Army from Fort Campbell knocks on my door and tells me that I am going to put up his troops for the night. Sounds right huh?" Silence.

"Instead of the Colonel, a police officer walks past my friend's house and thinks he may be doing something wrong. He knocks on his door and tells him, doesn't ask, tells him, he is coming into his house to look around. You with me Mr. Goball? Everybody else with me?" A universal nod, the jury still not figuring out where I was going with this.

"The officer then takes you down town and reads you your Miranda rights. You tell him you want to talk to a lawyer. He says, "Tough noodles', you don't get a lawyer. Doesn't sound like the America my friends, the WW II vets, fought for does it Mr. Goball."

"O.K. Mr. Goball, here is the punch line."

"I was wondering when you were going to get there?" A great laugh from all.

"Were you the student that the teacher always liked because you got right to the heart of the matter Mr. Goball."

"No, I was the class clown." I didn't doubt that.

"I'll give you that one Mr. Goball. But since you asked where I was going with this, here it is. Just as you wouldn't punish me for exercising my First Amendment right to free speech, or my or anybody else's First Amendment right to practice the religion of their choice, or my friends right to bear arms under the Second Amendment, or the right to be free from unreasonable search and seizure, and the right to not quarter soldiers, then Sissy has a fundamental right. Just as fundamental as all of the other Constitutional Rights I just enumerated. Know what it is Mr. Goball?" The class clown was speechless. Touché, you wise guy. Teach you to be a little leaguer in Yankee Stadium. Now make him feel good.

"Of course you do, Mr. Goball. It's Sissy's right to remain silent. She does not have to prove a thing. The Government has the burden of proof."

"O.K.", said Goball, "but don't you have to prove self defense?"

"Great question Mr. Goball. I sure do. Want to see how I'm going to do it without putting her on the stand?"

"You got me interested now Mr. Mills."

"You're my kind of juror Mr. Goball. You like reading mystery novels?"

"Not really."

"Anyone ever want to be a part in solving one, ladies and gentleman of the jury?"

They all smiled. Everyone wanted to do the right thing and believe they were the first to discover it.

Chapter 24

❖❖ Everyone likes to think they'll do the right thing when presented with a tough ethical enigma. Give the store clerk back the money when you get too much change. See the stranger drop her wallet and pick it up and give it to her and turn down the reward. The satisfaction of doing the right thing was reward enough. Jurors are the same. They genuinely want to do the right thing.

"The Commonwealth and I are looking for a fair and honest jury to stand between Sissy and the government, her accuser."

I hoped the jury bought into that paradigm and perceived me as the epitome of fairness. You had to convince jurors in voir dire that you were the one that was going to help them reach the right conclusion. Whenever, Simms comes into the courtroom, he lets the jurors that he represents all of the people of the Commonwealth. Jurors automatically identified with him because he convicted people who violated the law. Jurors obey the law, why can't the defendant? Simms was automatically the good guy. It's their job to help Simms send lawbreakers away. It was ethically the right thing to do. It was his job to remind them of this obligation, not to convince them of this obligation. Not a hard job to perform. My job, neutralize that paradigm and get the 'jury pendulum' swinging back to our side of the courtroom.

Goball wanted to stand up for the Constitution. All the jurors did. 'It was 'down right un-American to do otherwise.' I had to get them to check their natural inclination and leave their predisposition to believe Simms at the door, and go with the Constitution.

"Self-defense is an interesting point of law. Normally you, the jury, are instructed to judge the defendant's actions by what a reasonable person from this community would do under similar circumstances. In self-defense, you are instructed to look at the case from a subjective standpoint.

"Objective and subjective are two polar opposites." 'Oh that was great', I thought. 'That definition was no help. Now what? Think quickly while they are staring at you, waiting for a better example. Simms now sitting over at his table, knowing I was drowning in a sea of words and thoughts. A thought.

"How about this ladies and gentleman. One of your friends goes into the emergency room and tells the doctor he or she has just fallen from a tree and their arm really hurts. In fact, it's broken. The doctor takes an X-ray and says, 'your arm is broken.' Your friend's pain is subjective. He, the subject, can feel it. He does not need an x-ray to tell him he has pain. His or her body is doing a great job of that."

"But that's not good enough for the doctor. He wants objective, proof. Proof that the object, the arm, is broken. He wants scientific proof. Proof he can show you. Proof he can see."

I held up my arm like a doctor looking at an X-Ray, "He looks at the X-Ray and says, 'Yep, that puppy is definitely fractured.' Understand the difference between objective and subjective now a little better?" The group nodded. If one didn't nod I was going to go back and take another stab at making sure he or she understood. It was the major theme of the case last time when we tried the case the first time and I had to have Simms and his side of the courtroom on board that it was still the major theme. Tip my hand now and the house of cards came tumbling down and we would never found out who the courthouse connection was.

"When you look at the evidence regarding self- defense you have to look at it from Sissy's stand point. You don't get an X-ray to look into her brain, just look the broken arm from her standpoint."

Goball's hand went up.

"You and I are going to be great friends Mr. Goball." The jurors chuckled again. 'So much better than the jury from the first trial.' I was learning lots about this panel. At the same time I was educating them. Kurt, Emily, and Sissy, were all on the sidelines taking notes about jurors' nonverbal answers to my repartee with Goball.

"You always ask the most interesting questions and anticipate where I am going Mr. Goball." Now the jury was on my side as opposed to Mr. Goball's. Still, I needed him as a foil. Even if I couldn't strike him for prejudice.

"If she is not going to testify how do we know what kind of shape her broken arm was in? I gotta' hear her say 'Ouch!'

"You have any children Mr. Goball? Nieces or nephews?"

"Got two so-so kids and three wonderful grandchildren"

"No doubt. You ever see them fall from their bicycle, skin their knee, see them hurt themselves and say to yourself, ' Man that had to hurt. Here come the tears.'

"Got it." He said.

"You are with me on this one aren't you Mr. Goball. You judge what's going on around them and you make a judgment based on what you saw. You didn't have to hear them say ouch, did you?"

"I have to admit that at first I didn't know where you were going, or if I even liked what you were saying." He paused. "I didn't know if I even liked you at first, bein' a criminal defense lawyer and all."

"Got the same reaction from my wife on our first date Mr. Goball." The lady jurors really liked that one. Simms didn't like it. I was getting too 'schmoozie'. He had to feign a laugh to be on the jury's side. They were warming up to me. Nothing I was doing was objectionable. Simms had to sit there and take it.

God, sometimes I really loved this job.

CHAPTER 25

"There are some promises I need you to make Sissy. These are the same promises you would want your fellow jurors to make if a close friend or a family member of yours was on trial. Can you promise to try this case on its own facts?" Nods form all. "Everyone has their own prejudices. If there were a neo-Nazi on trial I would have to take myself off, me being Jewish and all."

"How many like George Bush's humor. Not "W's" but his father, Herbert Walker's?" 'Come on, I thought to myself, coaxing, raise your hands.' About half did. Sissy, Kurt and Emily wrote furiously.

"Remember he said he hated Brussels sprouts and they would never be served in the White House?" That's the kind of prejudice, or pre-formed opinion that Mr. Simms and I will talk to you about and ask you to get off the jury. Anyone got anything like that?" No one raised a hand. They were all fibbing to themselves and us. But I already knew that about them as humans.

"Now Mr. Goball he was not crazy about criminal defense lawyers. He had a pre-formed opinion about my practice and what I did. Still feel that way Mr. Goball?"

"Nope."

'You don't expect me to buy that bull shit Mr. Goball. You will be gone. But not because I used a peremptory challenge, but because the Commonwealth thinks we're buds. Thanks. You've made a great foil.'

"If you sit on this jury can you set those pre-formed opinions aside? Sissy has front teeth missing. You draw any conclusion from that? It's a pre-formed opinion. Set it aside. It is not evidence. Is everybody on board on that? Promise her if a fellow juror comments in deliberations on anything that is not in evidence you will remind them about this little talk we had?" Most nodded. It was the ones that didn't that drew my interest.

"Right now there are two people in this world that can control me. One is at home taking care of our children. The other is right behind me with the black robe and the gavel in his hand. Lord I hope that gavel isn't aimed at me. Is it Mrs. Smith?" She had smiled when I mentioned my wife controlling me. Just like the first trial, only now I was getting responses

"No you're lucky so far, but I think he has it cocked." Everybody laughed. I heard the black robe chuckle behind me.

"This is a really fun jury. Isn't it Mr. Simms?" I commented rhetorically. I liked them, and more importantly they liked me. The criminal lawyer's axiom was that a laughing jury was an acquitting jury. If they liked me they would like Sissy. Cognitive dissonance worked that way. At least that was what I was taught as Sociology major.

"Only those two can control me. Sissy cannot. If I do, or say, or if I have already said or done something to make you mad, hold it against me, not Sissy. Agreed?" The calm look of understanding emanated from the group. Next.

"Does anyone have any police officers in their family, say as close as first cousin?" No hands. "How about pathologists, ballistics experts?" Again, no hands went up. Then, a favorite question.

"Your honor," I said, turning to the gavel gripping one, "Defense accepts the panel." I had no alternative. But I had to make the public statement that I did. Who wants to hear 'I don't like you, but I'm stuck with you?' We went into the now vacant jury room to brainstorm and carefully take off three jurors that I could not get for cause. Each juror's unspoken agenda had to be figured out from the clues they had dropped.

CHAPTER 26

The mathematics to picking jurors after voir dire is not hard. You take the clues from their body language, divide by the number of smiles, and square the glares. Then use x-ray vision to look inside their brains based on the demographics, economics and gender. There were certain idiosyncratic principles I applied. I never let teachers sit on my jury, unless I wanted a one-person jury, which I never did. I'd bet on convincing twelve out of twelve rather than 'one juror takes all'.

In a sexual abuse case involving a twelve-year-old girl, I went with an almost all female because the defense was that the kid was a liar. The Assistant Commonwealth's Attorney thought I was nuts. Nine women? 'Better than fathers.' I thought. 'Who is more likely to believe that their little girl is likely to lie, a daddy who was wrapped around his daughter's little pinky or a mother who knew that their little girls could and would lie? The jury was out for twenty-three minutes in reaching the not guilty verdict. My client walked out of the courtroom with me. An innocent man I whom had kept off the witness stand and who had admitted to Social Services that he and touched the child's vagina through her underwear.

In requests for a big verdict an older attorney had advised me to pick poor folks for jurors. They liked sticking it to the rich. They pulled for the under dog he thought. My theory was just the opposite. Wealthy jurors understood that one hundred thousand dollars was not that much money. I got a six hundred thousand dollar plus verdict in applying my theory. Theories applied in science. Guess work applies in art. No rules applied in picking on jurors.

If you get it wrong in art just cover the mistake up with more paint. Take off or put more clay on the sculpture. In the jury selection you only got one shot. There was a gambling boat across the river from Paducah. I had been there twice. I gambled with people's lives every day. Are there higher stakes?

"OK Emily, who do you hate the most?"

"The oldest Baptist woman who had never touched liquor. She is going to love the fact that this happened at a par excellence red neck bar." We all agreed. One more strikes to use. Each now more valuable than the last,

"How about Goball people? A keeper or a chucker?" I asked

"My money is on Simms taking him off." Kurt said, "Simms' perspective will be that you and Goball are now good buds. Joking with each other and all. Let him waste one of his strikes. Then we can use our last one more productively." Kurt was right. Maybe. It didn't mater that Sissy and Emily agreed with him. Just because fifty million flies ate horseshit didn't mean it tasted good.

"How about we put him down as a possible and see where we are with the others?" Sissy sat there silently, now watching us argue and pick the people that would decide her future. I saw her and said, "Sissy, jump in any time. You see anybody look at you, you didn't like the look they gave you?"

"You guys are the pros."

"Look people, I don't need three yes men. If I wanted that I'd be doing this all by myself. You were looking at them while I was questioning them. Emily, you had the second row, Kurt, the third, Sissy the first. Tell me what you saw. What did you think their body language, or lack of it meant? Did they laugh when the others didn't? Were they disinterested and looking at the ceiling. In case you didn't notice Simms had a lot of people on his side of the courtroom doing the same thing. My intelligent friends, I need your intelligence. Simms is doing the same thing we are doing right now in his office only we have to do it better."

"OK, you want intelligence?" Kurt popped up, "I was watching Simms' people watching the jury and whom they were taking notes about."

"That's my bud Kurt. That's why you get the big bucks."

"I also saw them leaning in towards each other talking and nodding and shaking their heads about certain jurors, and pointing at the juror with their noses."

"You see Sissy, that's who you have working for you." She covered her mouth and smiled.

Kurt told us about the one's he thought they were pointing out. He saved us challenges. We would not know until the clerk drew the final panel if we were right.

After, thirty minutes of intense debate we had decided on the six that were gone. Goball was not on the list. There were other 'must strikes', but we had to take the crapshoot that Simms would strike some of the ones we were going to strike. Back in the courtroom the clerk took the names of the jurors we had struck from the box she drew their names out of. She shook the box and started calling out names. If we got it perfectly correct none of our strikes overlapped Simms'. The clerk called off the names of the final twelve jurors. The first eleven jurors called proved we were dead on. Then the twelfth name,

"Juror number 143, Mr. Goball."

Chapter 27

❖ The defense has two options when it comes to opening statements. You can go right after the Commonwealth or you can wait until the Commonwealth closed and you opened your side of the case. Only once had I reserved opening statements. When it came to Simms you were a fool to wait. The jury had to hear your side right after they heard his side.

Simms rose without notes and began. "May it please the court, Mr. Mills and most importantly, ladies and gentlemen of the jury. The Commonwealth will prove to you, beyond a reasonable doubt, that on November 28, 2003, the Friday after Thanksgiving Sissy Gilbert intentionally and wantonly killed Jeffrey Walker at The Valley bar. Those of you who don't know where it is, it's just before the Graves County line here in McCracken County. We'll put on all," emphasizing all, "of the people that investigated this case. At the Commonwealth's desk is Detective Olst with the Sheriff's office. He was the lead investigator. We'll put on everybody who saw what happened in the parking lot where the shooting took place, and everybody who saw anything in the bar before the shooting. We've got the coroner, the ballistics expert and the state pathologist who did the autopsy, proving that the bullet fired by Ms. Gilbert caused Mr. Walker's death. Now I want to tell you right now, Mr. Walker was no angel. He had his faults and foibles. The toxicologist will testify about the drugs in his system at the time he was killed. But that did not give anyone, including Ms. Gilbert, the right to kill him. Did it?"

Three of the jurors, including Goball, nodded in agreement. Sissy looked worried. She had seen him nod too. I had read him wrong. We had read him wrong, he had his own agenda. But he, like Simms, thought self-defense was the only defense.

"It's a simple case folks. Open and shut. After you have found her guilty we will go to the penalty phase and decide how much time she will have to do for this murder. Thank you." Short and to the point. A simple case needed a simple opening. I was going to reserve my opening, but that would have been different from what I had done in the first trial. I rose, greeted the court, Simms and the jury.

"Wow, you must think I'm a fool. No need to nod in agreement Mr. Goball." The other jurors laughed with me and, to some degree, at Goball.

"Well, I'm not a fool and this is not as simple a case as The Commonwealth would have you believe. The Commonwealth Attorney is sitting over there with pen in hand. I know this." I don't even have to turn around." The jurors looked over at Simms and saw that I was right. Four smiled. "He has his pen cocked because this is the first time he is going to hear about our case. It is your first opportunity too. Well let me tell you this. I think I got this one figured out and you and The Commonwealth are going to have to watch me develop Sissy's cases, and prove that the Commonwealth cannot prove beyond a reasonable doubt that Sissy killed Walker. Self-defense may not be the only defense. I'll tell you now she may not have been the only one with a gun in the parking lot at The Valley. Who did? Damned if I know. But I don't have to prove that. Ready to embark on the most interesting three days of your life? Me too."

I sat down and looked across at Simms. For the first time in my career I saw Simms look dazed. The rule on reciprocal discovery did not require I advise the Commonwealth of my theory of the case. Just a list of the experts and I intended to call. I had said nothing about Walker's history of violence. Olst stared his cocky; 'I dare you' smile. Simms called his first witness

Chapter 28

I thought Simms would call Olst to give the jury a thumbnail sketch of what had happened. Instead he called Ted Seller, the coroner. A coroner is a frustrated doctor. He always wanted to be a doctor but he just didn't have the brains to get into medical school. Instead he went to mortician's school. He still gets to cut up bodies, and look at the parts and tries to testify as to the cause of death. He may fill out a death certificate, but I never let him testify to the cause. He wasn't qualified and it pissed him off that I took away his chance to look like a physician.

After Simms does the name, age, address, occupation, elected official, schpiel; he got to the heart of the matter. The coroner testifies about what he saw and the condition of the body.

"Was Mr. Walker dead when you arrived at the scene?" 'He better be dead', I think to myself, 'or we're wasting a lot of people's time.' He really adds noting substantive to Simms's case, but crosses the T's and dots the I's that Simms needs to cross and dot.

"You may ask, Mr. Mills." The judge said as Simms went to sit down.

"Thank you your honor. Now Mr. Seller, did you take any measurements of the terrain?"

"No, I didn't think it was important. Do you, Mr. Mills?" He said, trying to be cute and get they jury to smile for scoring a point against an attorney in the attorney's own forum.

"There are a lot of things I think are important in this case that weren't done. I also find them interesting. I was hoping you saw this as more than your run of the mill homicide. But I guess you didn't"

"I take my elected position very seriously, Mr. Mills."

"You mean more than just seeing that you get re-elected."

"That's enough of that Mr. Mills." The judge interjected. I didn't know whether the jurors were smirking at my remark or at the judge chastising me. Truth be known, it was probably a combination of both.

"Why are measurements important in a case Mr. Seller?"

"What kind of case? What kind of distances? In a vehicular homicide they can tell you speed of the vehicle based on the length of the skid. A shooting." He paused. He just figured out where I was going.

"Yes, you were saying. In a shooting measurements can tell you what?"

"Well, it depends on what you are measuring?"

'The size of his schwanz, you schmuck; that's what you were supposed to measure.' I thought as I slid back to the podium, about fifteen feet from the witness stand, just to left of the jury box.

"Did you measure how far away Walker was from my client when the shot was fired?"

"No."

Did you measure the elevation of where Walker was standing on the porch to where Sissy was standing?"

"I don't think I understand the question."

"O.K. he is standing on the porch of The Valley. She is on the parking lot. We know how tall he is, right? Look at the pathologist's report. OK? We know how tall Sissy is."

"We do?"

"Sure, it's on her jail admission form. Now you see, we need certain measurements. Now do you know how tall Sissy is? How long her arms are?"

"No."

"Want to know why that's important Mr. Seller?"

I could see Simms leaning forward from his desk. Olst did the same. The Judge, gently rubbing the handle of the gavel against his lips, waited with the others for my answer.

"Yes I would Mr. Mills."

"Me too Mr. Seller. Stick around, cause when I figure it out, I'll let you know. But take this to the bank. I will figure it out. I may get there the back way, or backwards, but I will get there."

Chapter 29

"Mr. Mills, at the bench please."

"Yes your honor."

"I will not tolerate these histrionics in my courtroom. Do you have a defense theory in this case?"

"I think it may be self defense, but I'm looking at the case backwards now and I think I may have been wrong the first time I tried this case in that it is a case of self defense. But if and when I develop a different theory, I'll let everyone know, your honor."

"Mr. Simms?" the judge questioned

"Judge, it's all right with the Commonwealth if Mr. Mills wants to chase ghosts around the court room. I don't think the jury is going to be too impressed by the end if he has no more than a bass-akwards explanation.

"I appreciate the Commonwealth's indulgence, but I will try to get there your honor. After all, I have written a check with my mouth that I have to cash with my rear end your honor." The judge and Simms were silent. I took this as assent to my statement and stepped away form the bench and back to my podium

Measurements are important in science aren't they?"

"Yes they are." Now Seller knew not to screw with me. Answer my questions and get off the stand was his objective now

"Why?"

"Because they are empirical. Right"

"Yes they are. They cannot be changed. They are a constant. An ounce is an ounce, a pound is a pound. Correct?"

"Correct." I had him in a 'yes set'.
So, an angle is an angle and a height is a height.
Right?
Right'
And what can we determine from height and angle?
"I don't know Mills. What can we determine?" Impolite, dropping the 'Mr.' before my name. Now I was getting under his skin.
A lot. N'est pas"
What?"
Isn't that so?"
"It could be."
We can determine angle of trajectory. Right?
"I guess so."
"You guess so? How long have you been doing this job?
"About sixteen years."
"And how many courses do you take each year to stay qualified as a coroner?"
"The required, sixteen hours per year."
Sixteen per year to get better at it, times sixteen years that you have been on the job, six, carry the three, is roughly two hundred and fifty six hours. Figured you got it right yet?"
"Objection your honor, argumentative." inserted Simms
"Sustained." The black robed one dutifully blurted.
"I apologize if my math was wrong you honor. I was just trying to make a point." Simms and the judge had missed the point. A few jurors had not.
"When you approach a scene you don't know what happened do you? Or do you?"
"Well, I get the basics from the chief investigator, if that is what you mean?"
"I don't know what I mean. Sometimes when I ask a question. I just like to see where it leads me. You following me?"
He did not answer the double entendre.
"So, Detective Olst tells you what his investigation reveals, you plug that into what you find and think you have discovered without any measurements and you come to the same conclusion. Ever heard of a self-fulfilling prophecy?"
"A What?"
"You get out what you put in. In the military they call it GIGO."
"What?"
"Garbage In, Garbage Out."
"You insulting my work sir?"
"You insulted by my questions?" I answered.
"You don't answer a question with a question Mr. Mills."
"Why not?" I retorted.

The quick-witted members of the jury got that one. I turned and quickly tried to note which ones they were. Third on the right front row, last two on the left second row. Maybe I had three liking me. Maybe.

"Let me take another stab at this." Thinking that 'let me take another shot at this was not the metaphor I wanted to use.

"Detective Olst is first on the scene. He gives you information about the relative positions of Walker and Sissy, one on the porch one on the parking lot. You trust his information because you two have worked together before many times. Correct?"

"Correct.

"He is an excellent investigator. Your findings corroborate his finding." I've got him in a yes mode again.

"Correct?" I assert.

"Correct." He answers robotically

"But you don't know by your own measurements the relative angle of Sissy's gun to Walker do we."

"The bullet shattered the clavicle, collar bone if you will, and made a downward angle into his aorta. Thus it was impossible to tell the angle of entry."

"Impossible or not probable for you as a coroner."

"I don't understand the difference counselor."

His final assault on my line of questioning had failed. He did not know how pinned in he was to his own paradigm and how far away he was from my point.

"Are you a pathologist? An expert on ballistics after those two hundred and fifty six hours of training?"

"No."

"I guess that's why the Commonwealth has those experts. You pronounce them dead is all you do. Correct? You're not qualified to state the exact cause of death, that's the pathologists job correct?"

"Correct."

"And as a full time mortician, you just stuff 'em and mount 'em. Correct?"

I withdrew the question as Simms rose to his feet.

Chapter 30

I hadn't withdrawn my last question and the blacked robbed one had his gavel banging. The jury was still enjoying the end of my repartee.
"Approach Mr. Mills!"
Simms and I both approached. The only difference was Simms had a shit-eating grin on his face.
"Mr. Mills, you will pay a $250.00 fine for contempt by the end of the day or spend the night in jail, and you will apologize to this witness in front of the jury. Are we clear?"
"Yes your honor." I answered
"And it better be sincere. Correct Mr. Mills"
"Correct your honor." I stepped away from the bench and looked at Sellers who had heard the discussion at the bench and obviously looked forward to the public apology.
"Mr. Sellers, I apologize, sincerely, if I impugned your integrity as a mortician." The jury understood the inference. I was not apologizing for impugning his work as a coroner. I had given the black robed one what he wanted and still saved what I had gotten on cross. It was worth the $250.00. Truth be known, it was worth $500.00. If I was losing money on the case by the minute, why not go for it all?
My half-hearted apology had not gone unnoticed. Third from the right, first in the front row smiled trying to avoid eye contact with me. I walked toward my seat to await the rehabilitative re-direct.
"No further questions your honor. The Commonwealth calls Dr. Robert N. Rust."

The state pathologist, employed by the Commonwealth as a pathologist for more than fifteen years. I had questioned him before in murder cases. I had even used him as my expert in a wrongful death/medical malpractice case. If nothing else, he was smooth, a real charmer with the ladies. A doctor. Someone to be respected even before he entered the room. I had to turn him ever so gently to my side of the equation ever so gently. So gently even he did not see it. In Bridge they call it finesse. In trial I call it slick.

"Dr. Rust, would you tell the jury your name and occupation?"

"Robert Rust, Chief pathologist for the Madisonville crime lab."

"And how long have you been so employed?"

"Approximately fifteen years."

"Your honor, I will stipulate the witnesses credentials." Trying to save some of the impact of his testimony.

"The Commonwealth appreciates the offer, but feels it is in the best interest of justice that the jury get the full panoply of the doctor's back round."

His answer reminded me of Uncle Remus. 'Please don't throw me in the friar patch brother Bear. Please don't.' When that was clear to all that he wanted to be. Yeah Simms, throw me in the briar patch.

Simms ran him through his credentials from high school through residency, board certification and every medical society he belonged to. Then he got to the heart of the matter.

"Have you had an occasion to do an autopsy on the victim in this matter?"

"Yes I have."

"And have you reached a conclusion, based upon a reasonable degree of medical probability, as to the cause of Mr. Walker's death."

"Yes I have. It is my opinion that he died from exsanguinations."

"Can you tell the jury hat that means in plain western Kentucky language?"

The doctor smiled on cue. "He bled to death."

"And what caused that?"

"A projectile severed his aorta."

"How long did it take him to bleed out?"

"Conservatively, five minutes." Jurors loved to hear the word 'conservative' in a speech. In this part of American it somehow made them warm and fuzzy. Simms intentionally left out all of the gory details of the death. He left it to me to be insensitive in picking the dead body apart, a nice touch. A well thought out strategy. He was setting a trap and I was walking into it. Me do the high wire act in front of a tent full of circus goers.

Chapter 31

"Dr. Rust, I have had the pleasure of meeting you before haven't I?"

"Yes Mr. Mills, it was my honor"

"Mine as well doctor." I replied playing the 'who can brown-nose who more' in front of the jury more. "In fact it too was in a wrongful death case, like this one, only it involved a civil case against a physician and not a criminal case."

He nodded and waited for my next question. I had established at least some past history and some point of commonality in the judicial process.

"It seems to me there have been a number of facts left out of your brief direct examination and with your permission I would like to go over those if it is alright with you?" That's it; give the jury the impression that you are polite and well mannered. Always get permission. Even before you cut the witness' throat.

"There were a number of other scars on Mr. Walkers body weren't there?

"Objection your honor. This is not relevant." Simms said as he rose to his feet.

"Mr. Mills? The robed one asked.

"It is relevant to my client's perception of her need for self defense. If she or everyone in the community knew Walker to have a violent nature, as evidenced by his scars from various battles, then it is relevant."

"Mr. Simms?" The robed-one asked politely.

"Then lack of foundation. He has not laid the necessary groundwork to introduce this testimony.

"Mr. Mills?"

"I can lay the foundation."

"Then I will let it in provisionally. However, if a proper foundation is not laid, I may have to declare a mistrial. And they are expensive to the taxpayers, which expense may have to be re-directed Mr. Mills.

I understood the unveiled threat. Screw up and you pay cash for it and then get to start over again. Ah, what the hell, it was only $12.50 per day per jurors, fourteen, the usual twelve plus two alternates. Or worse, $12.50 times the entire panel that had been called in. Now that was expensive. I was already in the hole $250.00 'Go for it big boy' I told myself. Sissy, Emily and Kurt looked at me. I grabbed the first set of papers from the corner my desk. Emily reached into my attaché case for the others I was hiding

"Dr. did you find scars on Walker's body that preexisted this altercation."

"Yes, I did."

"Do you know the origin of those scars?"

"No."

"See your honor, no foundation." Barked Simms

"Two more questions for the foundation your honor, please."

"Two more Mr. Mills."

"Dr. I show you a certified copy of a Boyd County arrest and conviction of Walker for March 9, 2004. I also show you a certified copy of the Boyd County hospital for the same date."

"Objection your honor we have not seen these as required by the rules of discovery."

Your honor RCr 7,24 only requires that I made the documents available for copying. Mr. Simms sent Detective Olst to get a copy of my file didn't you?"

"I did." replied Simms

"And detective Olst always does what he is told to do doesn't he?"

Olst nodded. Only Olst, Emily and me\myself knew the answer to that question, and we were not going to rat him out. He had not done what he was told. He was too cocky and thought we had not done more work since the last trial. Simms leaned over to Olst. Then he gave him the harshest stare I had ever seen Simms give anyone.

"No objection." Simms muttered.

"What was Walker arrested and eventually convicted for Dr. Rust?"

"Felony assault first degree."

"And the time of the arrest?"

"8:36 p.m."

"And the time of admission to the ER?"

"8:55 p.m."

"And the extent of the injuries?"

"Lacerated liver, which required surgery, multiple stab wounds to various location of his body."

"What locations?"

Two in his left triceps, three in his right calf, one in this left thigh."

"As a forensic pathologist would you agree that it must have been one heck of a fight and whoever fought with Walker got in some good licks?"

"I would agree with that conclusion."

"And if Walker got charged and was not the victim he must have started it."

"Beyond my field of expertise. I'm just a doctor, not an expert like a lawyer." The jury chuckled.

"Very good doctor, I'll give you that one. How about this one?" He realized he should not have drawn first blood.

"Another certified record. This one from the Warren Circuit Court in Bowling Green Kentucky. What was the conviction there against Walker?"

"First degree Wanton Endangerment."

"You don't know if he was hospitalized as a result of that do you Doctor?"

"No, but I wouldn't be surprised if you didn't have another set of hospital records Mr. Mills."

Some jurors smiled. "Ah doctor, you are a quick learner. Perhaps you would have been a good candidate for law school." This time he knew not to get smart with me because I, of course had another zinger up my sleeve. "What were the nature of his injuries there, as evidenced form the Warren County Hospital records on the sane day and within an hour of the altercation?"

"One gun shot wound, grazing the left bicep and a stab wound to the left fore arm."

"Forensically a heck of a tussle?

"Probably so Mr. Mills." He had learned very quickly not to screw with me. He realized the sooner he got off the stand the better it would be for him and the Commonwealth.

"One last set off records Doctor." He looked relieved. "These from the local Graves Circuit court and the local hospital there. Again, felony assault, Walker gets hospitalized with in an hour of the fight. Serious injury to Walker?"

"Yes"

Because neither Simms nor the doctor had a copy of the Circuit Court records, they didn't know that the charges were pending at the time of Walker's death. It had to be a conviction to be admissible. But then again, I was not running a law school. My job- capitalize on my opposition's mistakes. I still wondered why Olst, even though he had not come to the office to copy our records, had not run an NCI on Walker. I imagine Simms wondered the same thing. Had he known about it he would have defused that bomb in voir dire. Dr. Rust's report showed all the scars, yet Simms had not discussed them on direct and Olst had made no effort to point them out to Simms by not getting the discovery from my file. They supported the self-defense theory. Someone was wanting me go down the self-defense path too confidently.

"No further questions your honor."

"Mr. Simms?" The judge asked, hoping he would rehabilitate the good doctor.

"Just one your honor, doctor, do any of those wounds warrant Mr. Walker's death in this case?"

I hit my feet before he got the words 'in this case' out of his mouth. "Objection you honor. That is beyond the pale of this witness' knowledge."

"Doctor?" asked the judge.

"Rust looked at Simms and then at me. He must have been asking himself if he wanted another fifteen minutes of me.

"I don't know your honor, I was not there."

"No further questions your honor." Simms said.

"Oops, just one you more your honor. I forgot to ask it on cross.

"Just one Mr. Mills." He cautioned

"You were not retained in this case to do the ballistics were you doctor?"

"No"

"That was a my one question your honor"

"Is the witness released Mr. Simms, Mr. Mills?"

"Yes your honor." Simms replied automatically

"No your honor. He is not released." Neither the judge nor Simms knew why I did not release the witness. Quite frankly, neither did I, but I had a hunch.

"You'll have to wait outside doctor." The robed on instructed

Chapter 32

Ballistics experts are neither a wan'na.-be pathologist nor a wan'na be surgeon. They want to be physicists. Truth be known, they want to be treated like they have a PhD. in physics. I think it's because eventually they go to gun school at Quantico, Virginia where all of the top-notch gun experts are trained, or because they are elitists. Either way, they demanded respect. No, they commanded respect. They let everybody in the courtroom, including the judge, that in their mind they were entitled to great respect. They are to bullets what neurosurgeons are to physicians, the best of the best.

"State your name and age for the record." Simms commanded, rather than ask. A clear subtle message that he was in control of the witness and not vis a versa. Obviously Simms had worked with her before.

"Val Chose, thirty-five."

She looked great for thirty-five and by the look on the faces of the men on the jury, they all agreed. I did not have to look at Kurt for confirmation. Emily, like most women, stared or glanced in reverse proportion to their degree of jealously. But whether male or female they were about to be wowed by her credentials, knowledge, and the ease with which she testified.

"And how are you employed?"

"As a ballistics expert with the Kentucky State Police."

"And how long have you been so employed?"

"Ten years."

"Tell the jury something about your back round."

"Your honor, I'll stipulate the witness is a ballistics expert." I offered hoping to take away some of her thunder.

'I appreciate Mr. Mills' offer again your honor, but I would like the jury to hear her eminent qualifications." Simms parried.

"I attended undergraduate school Eastern Kentucky University, where I graduated Magna Cum Laude in forensic science, my masters from University of Kentucky in physics and I have been accepted at the University of Virginia for my PhD. in Physics."

"Do you have any specialized training, Ms. Chose?"

"The usual training at Remington, Colt, and other gun manufacturers, training provided by the state in my internship and annual required training, and of course, FBI training at Quantico, Virginia." She said, non-plussed by her own credentials. "Also past president of the American Society of Ballistics and Forensic Ammunition Experts. I am a member of other societies within my field of expertise." She looked at Simms, dismissing his questions, nonverbally telling him to move on, she was bored with him and his questions.

He started to lay the foundation for the chain of evidence. Did so-an-so give it to you-know –who and then gave it to you, when I stopped Simms.

"Your honor, the defense will stipulate the chain of custody to expedite matters. This is not where the battleground lies in this case, your honor."

"Mr. Simms?" He asked, seeing if Simms wanted to speed up the process.

"Yes, your honor, that will expedite matters. Thank you Mr. Mills."

I smiled; creating the image of a get-a-long guy, send a message to the jury that I play nicely in the sand box with others. A considerate Yankee, was hoping for too much.

"Did you examine a bullet, that was sent to you, in this matter?"

"No sir." She paused for dramatic effect. "I examined the projectile. A bullet is both a projectile and a shell casing, so I did not examine a bullet."

Simms, initially shocked by the first part of her answer, let the three puckered sphincters in his body relax. I grinned. Touché toots, nice shot, no pun intended.

"Excuse me, the projectile. What did you determine from your examination, Ms Chose."

"The projectile had been fired from a .25 caliber pistol. Probably a Smith and Wesson or a Remington. There was a casing submitted to the lab so I compared the rifling on it to the .25 submitted." She proceeded to the next answer before the question was asked. "The rifling on the casing found at the scene matched the rifling casing from the .25 that was submitted to the lab.

"No further questions your honor. You may ask."

Simms was deliberately short with Chose because he thought knew where I was going to go with her from the first trial. He had seen the dog and pony show.

"Ms. Chase, a pleasure and an honor to see you again."

"Mine as well Mr. Mills." She retorted.

"About as well as anybody can about having to see a lawyer again," I smiled. She imitatively replied, the jury chuckled. They were starting to understand and appreciate my sometimes self-deprecating humor. Remember, I reminded myself; a happy jury is an acquitting jury. Even if the humor was at your own expense.

"The 25. Caliber projectile, was there any rifling on it?

"No."

I glanced at jury all of the women looked confused and wondered where I was going. The men were waiting for the next question. But I had to get the ladies on board. What was it the women didn't get? I got it- rifling.

"Can you tell the jury want rifling is?' The men looked at me like I was an idiot.

Chose explained. "As the projectile leaves the gun it spins. Because of the spiraling inside the barrel the projectile is scored. That is, as it turns the barrel makes grooves in the projectile. No two rifles leave the same grooving. It's like a finger print." I glanced at the women. They were now ballistic experts too and when they want back into the jury room and didn't have to rely on a good ole boy to explain it to them.

"So if there was no rifling how did you know it was a .25?"

"First the weight, second the size and third the back of the projectile. The bullet had been squashed, like a piece of old chewed bubblegum, squashed when it had hit a hard surface. The rear of the projectile was unchanged and thus .25.

Ms. Chose, what is the percentage of the female population that, if she carries a gun, it is a.25?"

"About 70 to 75 percent."

"Why a .25? Light, accurate, can be carried handily in a purse?" I interjected.

"Yes, but only licensed personnel should carry it concealed. She said with a wink in her smile headed in the direction of the women jurors. I smiled, thinking she was being coy.

"I guess the meaner the neighborhood the greater the need for protection?"

"Objection!" Simms said, quickly rising from his chair.

"Sustained."

I waited for the next motion but it never came. The motion instructing the jury to ignore the last question and answer." The jury though heard the objection sustained for an unknown legal reason, but I had gotten my point across. A lot of women, who carry, carry a .25

"As a ballistics expert, are you able to perform other tests?"

She knew where I was going and did not try to toy with me, as she had done at the first trial.

"You mean like the ability to determine angle of trajectory. The angle that the bullet travels from?"

"Where you able to make that determination?"

"No."

"Did you go to the scene?"

"Did the detectives give you the relative positions of Sissy to Walker?"

"No."

"Did you have the size of Sissy and the size of Walker and their weights?"

"The size and weight I got from the autopsy and the defendant's measurements from the jail web cite." For her, they were always defendant, not a name. Same psychological ploy I used, but inverted.

I asked, "Walker is on the porch of the bar the bar, Sissy is shorter, therefore she is firing up." "Correct?" "It hits his clavicle and then travels how?" "Down?" she answered.

"Yes? Does that comport with all of the years of learning that you have in physics?"

"Stranger things had happened Mr. Mills."

"Indeed, my very point. It could have come from another angle, another distance, because you don't have enough information to make that scientific determination.

She was starting to snarl. We had not gone in this direction in the first trial. But she conceded the point, with a nod.

"I'm sorry Ms Chase I need a verbal answer for the record. Was that a 'yes' to my question?

"Yes, it was a yes." But," she added, "Where is the other casing from the other projectile?"

"Casings that fall on the ground are easier to pick up than projectiles in a body aren't they Ms. Close?"

Chapter 33

You get breaks in life that you don't expect. Some call that grace. You get breaks in trial. Some call that luck. But at trial you make your own breaks. You work with witnesses to get their testimony comfortable, for both you and the witness. You research the law for a chink in the Commonwealth's armor. Every now and then you get a shocker, a witness for the opposition takes a quick glance at their moral compass, realizes that telling the truth is more important then the immediate gratification offered by the opponent and tells the truth. Just as I was expecting Simms to call Olst to tie up all the loose ends, from the previous experts he called Mulsum. The witness from Sissy's first trial that had taken a deal of the quasi-immunity the Simms had fashioned for him was expected to recant his testimony at the grand jury as a lie. Mulsum was again granted immunity if he told the truth, but Simms had to make the same deal with West. That was his interpretation of the Magnificent Seven's opinion, sauce for the goose, sauce for the gander. Simms had, what my Christian friends called, a 'come to Jesus meeting', what I called a 'come to Moses' meeting with Mulsum. Simms had woodsheded him so well; you could hear Simms testifying himself.

"Your name for the record please."

"Ralph Mulsum."

"And how old are you?"

"Thirty two next month."

"Where do you live?

"Around."

"Any specific address?

"Well, I can't fit in my mail box, so just around." Simms should have seen the sign, but he did not at first, and neither did I.

Were you at, The Valley Bar, the night that Walker was killed?"

"Believe so. Been a while, I think believe is as good as it's going to be for right now. A lot of beers that night, and then you have talked to me a lot about it too."

"I will use your testimony from the last trial to help you refresh your memory from the first trial.

"Suits me."

" I sense that you do not want to be here today, Mr. Mulsum. Is that correct?

"Lets just say this ain't my most comfortable place in the world." I loved it. A chink in the armor?

Did you see Sissy in the Bar that night?"

"Yep."

"Observe anything unusual about her actions?"

"Nope."

Simms did not like how this was going. He asked and received permission to approach Mulsum. "Do you remember your testimony from the last trial?

"Nope." Looking forward between my table and the jury, not wanting to make eye contact with anyone in the courtroom. Asked what he had done and maybe even what he was about to do.

Simms continued with his direct. "At the grand jury you testified that you did not see Sissy outside The Valley and that Ms. West drove off leaving Sissy there. Do you remember making that statement under oath?"

"Sure do."

"Still true?" Simms asked expecting a resounding 'Yep.'

"Nope." Mulsum said and crossed his arms defiantly waiting for the next question Evidently someone had not cocked and locked him. Lord knows it was not me.

"You are under oath and you are also subject to perjury charges if you testify differently from the first trial."

Mulsum stared at him. Either, he had thought his next answer through or he had consulted a sharp public defender. "The deal was, if I tell the truth, I would not be persecuted, if my word choice is correct, that if I testify truthfully I don't get tried. Right?" Simms could not leave it there. He had to have an answer and he needed it now. Simms answered Mulsum's question with a question.

"You lied at the last trial?"

" Yep." He crossed his arms even tighter. If they had been at The Valley they would have headed outside to settle it. But they were in Simms' forum, only verbal jousting allowed.

"Why the change, Mr. Mulsum?" Simms had better be ready for the answer. I know I was not.

"Walkers dead. Sissy's alive. But that don't matter. The truth is the truth. Since the last trial I been found. If I go to jail I can handle it. My Lord is with me." I guess the come to Jesus meeting had worked. But not for Simms. Simms had been set up. "I'm here to tell what I saw."

I looked up to see the jurors' reactions. They were as knocked out as I was. In voir dire, I had prepared them for this killer testimony that would hurt us. Was this an early Chanukah in Western Kentucky? My first gift was Mulsum? Should I send Simms a thank you card for the gift? A couple of months early, but who was I to look a gafilta fish in the mouth.

"O.K, Mulsum," Simms asked, now obviously dropping the 'Mr.' from the lead in of his question, "Lets hear what you have to say today then we'll go over where it differs from your grand jury testimony and the testimony at the last trial?"

"Suit ya-self Mr. Simms" Mulsum said getting politer, now loosening up on the stand, sending the jury the body language sign that he was now telling the truth and was comfortable with it. I clenched my pen. Kurt and Emily did the same thing. Sissy sat there and smiled, shielding her teeth from the jury. She had to be thinking that Carol would not have to testify. I knew better.

Simms staff didn't smile. They put their pens to their collective mouths. Some biting on the pen, some taping their teeth on them. The non-verbal clue was the same. They were not afraid of the answer. They were terrified, even breathless, at who was going to incur Simms' wrath for not letting him know this was going to happen. Simms walked back from the witness to his podium. He had his back to me but I could see the fear in the staff's faces as a mirror of what Simms had glared at them.

Mulsum began. "I got to The Valley about 9:00 p.m. got a beer and a shot of Tequila- Lime Salt on the side. Swallowed the Tequila, and threw the lime and salt on the floor.

I saw the usual Friday night crowd. But it was more crowded. Some of the preppies had returned to show off that they were in college. Hands not callused, ten years of grime under your fingernails missing. They were, what do you call it, 'Slumin."

"Did you stand in any one particular spot?"

"No."

"Do you recall testifying before the grand jury?"

"Yeah, I know what I told the Grand Jury."

"Then you lied the last time you testified?" Simms asked.

"I may have, but your immunity was for that time. The offer this time is for me to tell the truth. Therefore, if I lied either time you can't charge me with perjury. You call in law. Collateral, somethin'."

"Estoppel" I inserted.

"No, my lawyer told me it had something with contract law and equality, make an agreement and the government has to be bound by it. I had a piece of paper with cases written on it, but I l lost it. It had the name of a candy bar and being heavy. That was the way I tried to remember it. Guess it didn't. The jury chuckled.

"Clark v Burden.' I interjected, dyslexically putting the crossword together. Did he know Workman?

"I will prosecute you Mulsum."

"Your honor how is this material to the present case?"

"Can't do it, don't care if you do. Truth is truth." Repeating the mantra taking on a Friday night Valley Persona. He may have been saved, but like most, when in a corner he resorted to what he knew best.

"And tell me why."

"'Cause my lawyer said, and I hope to God he is right or else I do time and he has to call his malpractice insurance company."

"And that Attorney was?"

"Objection your honor, irrelevant and that information is privileged and the witness should be instructed by the court about it.

"Ladies and gentlemen of the jury, now is as good a time as any to take a fifteen or twenty minute break. The attorneys and I have some evidentiary matters to discuss that you do no need to hear. The usual admonition about people talking to you still applies. With that, I'll see you back here in 20 minutes. Counselors, approach."

"Mr. Simms, I can tell that this jury is confused and frankly, so am I."

"Judge I'm allowed to impeach his testimony by a prior inconsistent statement."

"You are introducing evidence to contradict your own witness' testimony and try to prove the negative? Correct?" I nodded in agreement. Rule one was now working to my advantage.

Your honor, this is a complete surprise to me." Simms pleaded.

"Well, you have eighteen and a half minutes to research and tell me why I should not stop your questioning, about what he and his attorney talked about, and even who that attorney was, that is all, gentlemen."

Simms scrambled to his office. The assistant Commonwealth attorneys had already started the research before Simms got there. He literally hit the door on his way out of the courtroom.

"You and you, do the research and it better be right on point. Olst, you come with me and tell me who cocked Mulsum. Everyone thought that Simms had interviewed Mulsum himself, just as he had done in the first trial. Tell the boss he screwed up? Not a pleasant thought.

"Bring me the work sheet and see who was assigned to Mulsum's interview, heads will roll people," Simms barked

A paralegal went into the courtroom and retrieved the assignment sheet. On the left side of the column of names were the initials of the assistant assigned to interview the witness. She returned to the office and went to hand him the list. He grabbed it from her.

"Here, now I got it. And the winner of a lost job is in this office is...." Simms said noting else and told Olst who had left the room to stop. Simms went behind his desk and cradled his chin between his interlocked fingers, watching the associates work through the millions of citations for the most appropriate case. At exactly eighteen and a half minutes Simms and the jury walked in. He approached the bench as the judge settled into his chair.

"Well Mr. Simms?"

"<u>Commonwealth</u> v. <u>Overlord</u>, a 2007 case. Unpublished, but on point. Therefore the court can interpret it's understanding of the law based on Overlord."

"Mr. Mills?"

Oh yeah, like I had all of my research resources available here, a definite down side to solo practice.

"Mr. Mills have you read Overlord?"

"I got it handed to me your honor at the same time you did." The robed one had not read it. He trusted Simms' interpretation. "Please excuse me. I'm dyslexic and I'm a slow learner."

"You rely on that dyslexic crutch too often Mr. Mils."

"Just when it applies your honor." I wondered when reality became a crutch. Those who had never been afflicted with any disorder could not fathom the all consuming little 'reading and writing' problem. I read Overlord and saw that no matter what I said, the issue of whom he had talked to was coming in. What they discussed was not coming in. That privilege was still intact.

"Your honor, I would withdraw my objection as to who Mr. Mulsum talked to if you would instruct now and at closing that they can give Mr. Mulsum's testimony the weight they choose to."

"Ladies and Gentlemen of the jury, I must instruct you as follows." He quoted my request almost verbatim. Simms prepared to strike.

Chapter 34

"You sir, are a prevaricator." He began, giving each word its own emphasis.

"I ain't never touched an animal in that way." The jury could not stop laughing. They may not have known that a prevaricator was a liar, but they knew it had noting to do with bestiality. The answer rattled Simms. Lord he was not having a good day.

"It means you are a liar."

"Ain't the first person to do it in this case." He muttered just loud enough for me and the jury to hear.

"I maybe done a lot of things and I may not a made a lot of good decisions, but I am what I am, a simple country boy, who was in the wrong place at the wrong time to see something that didn't involve me, wish it was otherwise." He looked up to see the jury's reaction to be distracted by the twelve-foot doors opening into the courtroom. The doors creaked open. The jury was no longer Mulsum's concern. Simms backed off. Mulsum's humble act was garnering sympathy for Sissy. Maybe she was being picked on after all.

I heard the 12 foot oak doors close and looked back. "Well, Look who decided to show up." I whispered to Kurt and Emily. They both nodded. Emily took out two of the stock subpoenas we had in attaché case and handed it to Kurt. There was only one piece of information missing on the subpoena. The witness' name.

"What do I tell her?"

"Hold on." I whispered again, "You get your butt outside the courtroom and be ready for her to leave. You grab her and serve her. Got it?" He did and rose and left by the side door so he could grab her as she exited the back door. As I approached the bench I saw her sit down in the back. Not knowing what was bout to happen. Your honor, the rule has been invoked. A witness for the defense has just entered the room and we need to exclude her before another word of testimony is adduced."

"What's the witnesses name Mr. Mills?"

"I'll tell her your honor." I walked past the jury box and pointed to the blonde. "Miss, you are going to have to leave the courtroom. You may be a witness for the defense." She looked to the front of the courtroom for instruction and got none. She shrugged and left by the back door

Kurt, as usual, was brilliant. He told her he had a subpoena for her and needed to see her ID to make sure she was over twenty-one. What he really needed was her name on the subpoena. He got it

`"What happened?" I asked with my arched eyebrows

"I served her of course."

"Why the long face? You done good man. Did you tell her about the Rule."

Real plain on that point. Told her twice and was about to make it a third when she interpreted me and said, "I get it."

She stomped off heading down the hall."

"Which wing?

"West. Why?" Kurt looked interestingly

"Simms office is down there.

"So is fifty percent of the court house staff, your point?" Kurt wondered.

"Don't know as I have a point, but boy I sure better get one or Sissy's ass is back in a sling."

Simms was now handling Mulsum with kid gloves. Simms had made his deal with the devil and now 'he had to dance with the girl what brought him to the dance'. This made my planned twenty-five minutes of cross-examination turn into five minutes of playing nicely in the sand box with the new kid on the block.

Simms was allowed to treat Mulsum as a hostile witness so there were leading questions galore.

"So you are telling this jury that you lied under oath before the grand just and now you are telling the truth?

"Right."

"Why should they now believe you? You were under oath then too weren't you?

"Yes."

Going on like this for each contradiction between his grand jury testimony and his testimony today. You have to know when you reach the point of overkill. Simms overkill detector was obviously broken. He, like my father, had thought that the louder and the longer you spoke the more the correct your position became. You were not beaten into submission, you were bored to death. The orator, confusing one for the other.

But evidently Simms' staffs' overkill buttons were working. The attorney sitting in second chair passed Simms a note. He asked for a moment from the bench and got a waive of the hand in response. Ten seconds later Simms had no more questions. He was done with Mulsum.

"Mr. Mulsum we have met once before and have not seen each other since that date in court a couple of years ago have we?"

"Sure haven't. Good Lord's been good to me."

I chuckled in tune with the jury and retorted, "If you're going to the doctor or the lawyer this is generally not a good thing.

"Can we talk about truth for a moment Mr. Mulsum?"

"Sure."

"Truth is a constant, don't you think?"

"I guess?" He paused, " What's that mean?"

"It means that it is always right on the mark. If you are target practicing for bow season you want the arrow to be on the mark. The bull's eye is always the bull's eye. The truth is always the truth. We may think we are aiming at and hitting the truth, but really only truth determines if we are telling the truth." I really lost him the jury and me with that one, "but I digress."

"As long as I don't have to repeat what you just said I'll be fine." Mulsum smiled.

"I'm not going to use words like 'prevaricator' or other derogatory terms. I want to talk about words and thought." Shit, here I am teaching. Teaching existentialism for the in-bred.

"We chose the words we need to sometimes based on where we are in our life. Isn't that right?" He listened. "Lie when you were in the grand jury. Everybody was nice to you. Mr. Simms was please to see you, introduce you to the grand jury members and probably even offered you coffee and a donut."

"Yeah, it was real nice. So? What are you implying?"

"Nothing, just trying to understand where you were. I know the who, the when and the where. Now we just need the why, and I think the same truth we are both looking for will work for us. So let's try shall we? Promise it won't hurt. Just trust me. I had his attention and it was razor sharp.

"I'm just saying your human, not like lawyers." He smiled I could not miss the self-deprecating shot. Because, every time they laughed at me they re-examined the Commonwealth's case. Humans do that.

"O.K. So I'm like everybody else." He said

"Kind of comforting isn't it?

"Yeah."

You told Mr. Simms what you thought he wanted to hear. That Carol did give Sissy a ride, right? But when it got down to the real nitty gritty, when the truth had to come out, making people feel good wasn't that important was it?

"No." He slumped sheepishly. Now to pick him up out of the doldrums and show him he was a hero.

"But you just did the heroic thing, you stood by the truth. Because you knew it was more important than anything you might face. Even if it meant having to confess your little tale in public. Someone's life was and is on the line and you realized the importance of the constant. The truth." He looked up from his sweating palms.

"Yeah, that's what I did."

"And that's why we know that you are telling us the truth today isn't it."

"Yeah."

I almost asked for an 'Amen.' from the jury but thought that was reaching. But then again, there were the Baptists on the jury. "You saw Sissy leave with Carol West. Didn't you?"

"Yeah."

"You were out there before Sissy and Walker got out there weren't you?

"Yeah"

"We really don't care why you were out there, burning one, snorting alone, but you were out there." He did not answer. "You saw the shot."

"No! He jerked, I heard them."

"Them?"

"Yeah. I guess an echo; you know how the Valley is in a cave like place."

"How far apart were the echo's?"

"Hell, I don't know counselor, I had been at the Valley for hours. I heard them and saw the flashes on the clay wall.

"Light echoes Sir?"

"Yeah, you know, like light bouncing around."

Maybe I did want to know what he was consuming out there. The jury glanced and waited for the question. I didn't ask it because I would have to admonish him not to answer it because of his Fifth Amendment right and I had already danced that jig with the judge.

"No further questions your honor."

"Subject to re-call your honor." Simms monotone to the bench.

"You'll have to wait outside me. Mulsum." The judge instructed.

"Ladies and gentlemen, it has been along day and I think this would be an opportune time to take a break. We will adjourn for the day and I will see you here tomorrow bright and early at eight forty-five a.m. You are dismissed with the usual admonition and I want you also to not read or listen to any newscast about this case.

Sissy looked at us for direction. I looked at Kurt.

"What is her name?"

He whispered the name to me. "Jackie St. Clair"

"Never heard of her. You checked her I.D.?" I asked. He nodded

"'What you doin' for breakfast tomorrow morning?"

"You tell me." He said without having to whisper, now that the judge was gone and we were packing our stuff for the night.

"Meet me at The Valley for ham and eggs at about 4:30 a.m."

"They're closed at that time." He protested

"I know but let's see it at 4:30 before the sun rises. No one will be there. Bring the .25 you have strapped to your left calf and I'll bring my equipment.

"How you know I got a 25 there?" Kurt wondered.

"I don't, but I know you."

Chapter 35

❖❖ The Valley at 4:45 a.m. is interesting and unusual. The usual three to five cars whose drivers had been given or asked for a drive home. The lights were off. It was Wednesday morning following a slow Tuesday night. They had probably closed up early. But a 4:30 rendez vous assured there would be no one there. And with deer season at its peak, no one would think the sound of a gunshot was out of place. Kurt pulled up just after I did.

"Morning."

"Is that what this is?"

"Best part of the day. Quiet. Good for concentrating."

"Do you know there is nowhere to get coffee at this time of the morning coming from Mayfield."

"This won't take long."

"You got the .25?" Silly boy, of course he did. Probably has two and a .357. Kurt you stand where Sissy was standing, pretend to shoot Walker, when I say. I walked back for the scene to see it from the road to see if it was as close as possible to an actual re-creation. 'Looked good,' I muttered to myself.

"OK Kurt, kill the mother."

He pulled the trigger once. There was an almost imperceptible echo, but something was missing. 'What had he said?' 4:45 a.m. and I was playing the trial version of trial double jeopardy.

"Yes, Alec Trebec, I'll take testimony for two hundred. Who was the last witness and what is a flash and an echo. Correct Tim, pick again."

"Kurt, stay there. I'm going back to where Carol West's car was." I shuffled across the gravel parking lot, dusting my shoes with dense-grade gravel dust. Man, that stuff was tough to get out of the corners of the toes of your shoes.

"O.K. Shoot that mother again."

The .25 was unmistakable. The echo in the clay pit was much worse the by the road. No wonder no one heard the shot by the bar's front door, closest to the road. But Carol heard the echo and Mulsum saw an echo's flash. Undoubtedly, a function of too many combinations of substances, on both sides of the law. Hell, down here the moonshine, could make you hallucinate, LSD with meth? A nice cocktail, pot and anything else, hell the possibilities were endless.

"Take your .357 out and fire it." Kurt looked at me unbelievingly. Did I want the police here for sure? He complied. ' Much too loud.' I thought to myself. "I pulled the .25 I kept in my office and told Kurt to look my way. I fired just above the roof of The Valley. "What did you see and hear?" He looked at me with awe. From the look on his face I knew he knew, what I now knew for sure.

"It was a second shot, close to West's car. But, who and why? We've got the what, when and where."

"A wise young psychologist once told me to not concentrate on the why. It would come by itself?"

"O.K. Mr. Wizard, we proved the echo of the flash was a second shot. Did West fire it? The blonde fire it? Someone other than the blonde? The guy on the grassy knoll?" Kurt said, mocking my obsession with the JFK shooting.

"We know that light travels more quickly than sound." I stated.

"4:30 a.m., a little early for a third grade physic lesson."

"Remember what you heard and saw. I'll probably have to put you on the stand." Kurt nodded his understanding. It was not a scientific test, but it would meet the evidentiary test to be admissible. We drove off toward McCracken County, stopping at the first greasy spoon we saw.

"Eat up Kurt, it's going to be busy day." I usually ate only breakfast when I was in trial. Lunch was spent going over the morning's trial notes and plugging them into the closing argument. Dinner was a double Dewar's. I needed to get on grasp on that part of my trial meal I noted to myself, but today was not that day. We talked about anything but the trial. Although not crowded, there were people in close enough proximity to worry about. I recognized a singular pain the big in my fright foot. It was unmistakable. Every gout attack I suffered started with this twinge. I excused myself, went to the car and got out seven five milligrams of prednisone, the silver bullet for all gout and arthritis sufferers. Few physicians believed that stress caused gout. Those of us that suffered from it knew otherwise. I had to keep them in my mouth, until I got back into the restaurant. That would be all I needed for the people in there, to see- me popping pills before trial, could have been Flintstone Vitamins. It didn't matter. Again, the perception was greater than the reality.

""Man, those son-of-a-bitches are bitter."

"Gout, got your goat?" Kurt alliterated.

"I wouldn't wish this on the man behind the bench."

"That bad?"

"Worse. And I can't take anything narcotic for the pain." I could tell from how this attack was starting that even a Lortab or two would not touch this pain. And it was going to get worse before it got better.

"Oh you are going to be a joy at trial today."

"It will keep me on point." I said through my now clenched teeth.

"Now Simms, on the other hand, I would not mind passing it on to him.

"Getting personal now, counselor?" Kurt said, holding his napkin to his mouth to avoid showing me how he masticated his meal.

"You think we wrap it up today?"

"If Simms loses his voice, or puts on Olst and rests. He may try short and simple this time rather than long and boring, although the later had worked last time. But this time he knows, we have another theory. He may want to get me to my case right away and then disprove it in rebuttal." I bought breakfast. We headed to the office to go over his testimony, now that I had to put him, on the stand. But, how to get around the fact, that he had been in the courtroom, in violation of the rule.

While running him through his proof, I went through the rules of evidence. After he was cocked and locked, I turned around and hit my research engine, to get case law to back up my position. I had to be spot on. Anything less would fail, and get Sissy convicted.

Chapter 36

 "McCracken County Jail, may I help you?"

"Yeah, Jiggy? I said recognizing the voice. " This is Tim Mills, and that's not your fault. Did they bring in Carol West last night from Vandenberg County?

I heard him chuckle at he first line. "Not supposed to tell you Tim. Does that answer your question?"

"Thanks Jiggy, I owe you."

The drive to jail was short, but not short enough. West would not be happier to see me now. She had gone from friend to enemy. I had to figure out how to get her back onto the friend side of the equation. Now I knew, what she knew, and she didn't know that I knew it.

Again, an amorphous voice from the jail intercom answered.

"May I help you?"

"Mills to see Carol West." The latched clicked opened the door. I pushed the door inward. The jailer met me at the door.

"We don't have a Carol West here, Mr. Mills."

"Says who?"

"Says me."

"Well, I say that she is here and if I find out that she is here and you denied me access to her before trial then I am going got go to the paper. Not the Commonwealth Attorney, to get you indicted for obstruction of justice. I will ask the reporter to explore the reasons that the jailer was a co-conspirator to obstruction of justice, denying my client access to a key witness, and helping to hide her. That's not what you are doing; is it?"

"No, just following orders."

"Whose?"

"Someone with a lot more authority that you, counselor."

"Who?"

He walked away from, me and then turned abruptly "You need to leave. Now! You were never here."

"I am, I have been, and I will be. It's a *Vini Vidi Vici* kind of thing. Besides, the jail video shows me coming in."

"Didn't I tell you the video was broken?" he said, trumping me.

"You got control of the Vandenberg County jail log, or the 911 tape of the deputy calling into 911 with the mileage and time that he was leaving Indiana with West? Now I'm going to call Simms at home and wake him up. If I don't wake him up I'm going wake up the judge. Hell, he's already up to my transverse colon. A little further is not going to hurt me. And I'll bet you whoever I call will tell me, that they never told you not let me see Carol West, that will leave you out to dry. Not only out to dry, but alone and screaming that it is a conspiracy to get you just like a lot of your inmates. Not a real comfortable thought now is it? "Haven't quite thought this all the way through have we?"

He just looked over my balding head. Did I really have the stones to pull this off? I could watch him weighing my past history of writing checks, with my mouth, that my rear end could not cash against his future as a jailor making just over six figures a year housing society's pumpkin suits. I reached for my cell phone. He looked down at his clipboard.

"No shit, I think they just brought her in. Of course, we have to get her checked in, showered, fed, and clothed and ready for her big day. Could take five to six hours to get that done."

"Screw with me. Just go ahead and screw with me." I quietly screamed.

"Can do, counselor." Sensing that he had me.

"You remember Watergate?"

"Yeah."

"You learn any lessons form it?" He just stared at me "You know, the one thing I learned from Watergate was to assume that no matter where I was, there were others there who would not put their ass on the line for me. Paranoid or worried now?"

"Maybe, just a little bit of both."

"A bad combination, huh?"

"Maybe not. You remember the donuts?"

"Damn, I knew I forgot something. Next time I'll double up."

He lead me into the interview room, turned the T.V. onto the Weather Channel, up really loud and pulled me into the TV.

"Now you listen to me, you little Jew Lawyer. You can pull this shit other places, but not in here, this is my kingdom. I'm thinking you are a pawn. You don't know who you are fucking with. You have no idea who you are fucking with. You don't even want to know. Trust me, I know and you don't want you know."

I grabbed his arm right arm on the inside of his bicep right where it meets the triceps and pushed my thumb through to the shoulder. Speechless, he cringed.

"Now you listen to me you old Nazi fart. I will crap on your grave with my kosher turds long after this is over. You bring me West safe and warm, and I will let you go and eat your morning grits." We smiled at each other for the video camera in the room. He walked away shaking his right arm.

"Carol! Really, great to see you."

"I thought you were Simms or someone from the Commonwealth to get me ready to testify. I'll give him whatever he wants just to get out of this freakin' place."

"Maybe not, after what you hear what I have to say."

"Ain't nothing you got that I'm interested in. Sissy is on her own. What she and me had is over. Never was and never will be. She can go back to Peewee Valley. Her problem. She is out of my life."

"It wasn't the fact that you gave her a ride home that they are afraid of."

"What you figure you got figured out, counselor? Because I'm goin on the stand for the Commonwealth and then I'm out of here. No bond, no charges, free from the material witness warrant. Free, free, free."

"My second favorite word that begins with the letter "F" Carol'

"And I know what the first is."

"Yeah, begins with an F and ends with a "K:"

"You got it. I love to eat and it is 'fork', and you thought it was the other word."

"Who wouldn't?"

"Yeah, right. But that is my point. Sometimes we assume we know what the other person is thinking and we don't. They give us clues and we just see what we want to see. You give Sissy a ride but it is not the ride that is significant. It was the echo. It was not an echo. It was a second shot. And where was it fired from? You know and if you tell you are an after-the-fact conspirator to murder. You know who fired the shot and were about to 'do her'. You were headed home with her. Right? I've got the when and the where. Now I just need the who and the why. Then I may know the what."

"Well, counselor you don't have much time. I'm set to testify for the Commonwealth and then I'm gone."

"Not so, Ms. West. Here is my subpoena to appear. You will stay until I am done with you. I got the court order from Vandenberg and you are not gone until I am done with you."

She looked down at her prison orange sneakers. "O.K. maybe you got it now what do I do."

"You tell the truth."

"Yeah the whole truth, blah, blah, blah."

"You heard what you thought was an echo, but it could just as well could have been two shots correct."

"I guess."

"No, I need for you to be sure on that point."

"O.K. I'm sure I can guess on that."

"Don't play with me."

"Don't try to put words in my mouth and get me to commit perjury. I got enough people tryin' to do that?"

"Who?"

"Who do you think? That bald headed cop who drove me down here from Vandenberg and schooled me the whole way down. Hear the echo, gave Sissy a ride, don't testify to anything else. Just like the last trial. No one knows any different if my testimony remains the same. Verdict remains the same. Who is hurt?"

"All you testified to the last time was that you gave Sissy a ride home. You testified that Walker pushed Sissy, and you talked about the echo. What you didn't talk about was the fact that it wasn't an echo. It was a second shot fired from behind you or beside you. You saw who it was and now I know who it was. It was the blonde, St. Claire." I looked into her eyes to see her reaction. It was blank.

"Who is St. Claire?" she asked

"We have her under subpoena to be at trial."

"Describe her." She said.

"Blonde, probably a wig. Store bought 38 DD's. Five foot two inches, five foot three inches. Great legs. That her?"

"Yeah, that's her, but not her name. I don't know what she told you or that idiot Polish P.I., but her name is not St. Claire. And if you don't have the right name on the subpoena you got shit, right?"

"But she showed Kurt her I.D?"

"And you think someone that well connected doesn't have several I.D's? Not only are you dyslexic you're not real bright. You ain't got shit and I ain't talkin' about anything other than what I saw the last time, not some screwed up theory of yours.

Or anything else."

"Pick your friends, pick your poison Carol, but just for my own sanity. Have I got it right?"

"I heard two shots and saw the shooter. There wasn't an echo. The second shot came from behind me. Not, next to me. I wasn't in on the shootin' if you were thinkin' I was. I may love women, but I ain't no thief and I ain't no killer. Although I do like women who are killer lookin'. When I heard it, I turned around to see, who had fired the shot and where it had come from. I did not see the person's face, but it was the only person that looked like that, at The Valley that night."

"The blonde?" I asked. She nodded, affirmatively.

"It looked like she had been waiting for Walker to come out. When I turned she had her arm against the Lincoln to steady her shot. She turned to shoot me, but I grabbed the ground. That's when Walker said, "Damn Sissy, you really shot me." Evidently, she did not have enough time to pick up the casing from her .25 and shoot me and leave. I guess she just got lucky that Sissy was out there because she was going to kill Walker anyway. Proof that the golden rule even applies to luck. Doesn't it. Mills?" Then she drove past us throwing dust and stopped and pointed her finger at us and pulled the trigger on her index finger with her thumb. Sissy and me got the message."

"Anything else?" I probed.

"You ask, I'll talk." She answered. "That's all I got. Sissy ran over to the car, got in and we left."

"Did Sissy see who it was?"

"How could she? I told her and that's how she knew to keep her mouth shut."

Chapter 37

"Exiting the jail, I realized how many levels there was to Sissy's statement. I knew what she had done, or did I? I opened the last door from the jail and looked up.

"Simms, what are you doing coming over here? You are persona non-gratis here. A dangerous place for you. Not a lot of friends of yours in here.

"Not interested in friends, just a witness. What you doin' here, Mills`?"

Seeing Sissy before trial." The head jailer wasn't going to rat me out, he had violated Simms' or someone else's order and was not about to rat himself out.

He was going also make sure that no deputy jailer got to Simms to rat him out either. Carol was not going to rat me out either. Like a good pistol, she too, was cocked and locked. And, if she backed up, I had backup. Let Simms talk to her and get her cocked and locked his way. One of us, was going to be surprised, and if I played it right it was not going to be me.

Snapping my finger loud enough to make sure Simms heard it, I pivoted in the ball of my right foot, forgetting that I was fighting the onset of gout. I cringed.

"Gout?" Simms inquired. "Disease of the rich, a bunch of bullshit, Mills?"

Simms cringed. He was a good Wednesday and Sunday church going Baptist and did not care for swearing. According to him, curse words were the adjectives of the uneducated. I countered, never underestimate the power of words to get your point across, and that in my end of the business you had to speak 'street'. Actually I enjoyed watching him cringe. Like my gout, it was an unexpected pain. Certainly, one he did not expect, from a fellow member of the bar."

"I know there was something I forgot to ask Sissy." Getting to the point of my pirouette, sometimes I think that if brains were dynamite, I couldn't sneeze."

The buzzer, buzzed and let us in. Sure as God, made little green apples, the head jailer met us. He quickly glared at me. I winked back as friends wink and nod.

"You forget something with Ms. Sissy, counselor?" He asked.

"Sure did." He knew exactly why I was back.

"And what bring the Commonwealth Attorney here? Normally if you interview a witness you have them brought over to your office."

"Special circumstances." Simms retorted.

"Who you need, Mr. Simms?"

Simms handed him a note with a name and a couple of short sentences written on it. It's amazing what you can see in the jail with all the bright lights if you keep you eyes open. It was backwards, but I could translate it.

"You got it Mr. Simms. Mr. Mills, you go to the usual spot I'll get you yours."

"See ya." I said to Simms

"Yeah, you too. Later." Said Simms

"Well, Sissy, I see you're the usual up beat person today."

"Oh, yeah, real excited. You think this will be over today? I'll have to start all over again at Peewee Valley to work my way up to a better bunks."

"Have I ever told you about my favorite word that begins with the latter 'F' and ends in the letter 'K'."

"Yeah like what is about to happen to me.

You going to eat because the word is 'fork' not what you were thinking. See you assumed that you knew what it was. Sometimes you have to think differently than others. Carol missed the test too.

"You talk to her?"

"You know it."

"She is going to tell it all?"

"No, but the good news is that I figured it out. Now I just have to figure out how to prove it, and keep you off the stand. Know what my second favorite word is that starts with the letter 'F'?"

"The one I just thought of the first time?" She half-smiled.

"No. Wrong again Sissy. It's 'Free'."

"Free?" She said, "All I got to do is two years to the board. They flop me for a year and then I'm free. If she ain't testifying to the truth that is the only way I get free."

"You can't testify to the shadow of the person Carol saw behind the car because that would be hearsay because she told you what she saw. You get it? You did not see it yourself, and of course she will deny saying it. And there we are, with an unsubstantiated conspiracy?"

"At least in four years, I'm still alive. You really don't understand the power people have, do you Mr. Mills?"

"No one has that much power."

"That's freakin', what's the word?" She asked.

"Naïve?"

Chapter 38

As pissed off as I was, I still had to be the penultimate gentleman in front of the jury. Pulling her chair back for her when we came back from breaks, or when ever she came back. Leaning over to talk to her and smile like we were having a real pleasant conversation, when all I was saying to her was, "Act like we are having a pleasant time when I pull away, look at me and smile and make sure the jury sees it." She nodded her understanding. I pulled away as, she smile covering her smile enough that you just could not see her smile;"

"All rise." Everyone stood up for the man in the black robe. Not that I wanted to, but it was a sign of respect for the court, not the official. I kept reminding myself of that every time I had to stand for him.

"Counsel approach."

"Good morning your honor." Simms and I said simultaneously.

"How much more for the Commonwealth?"

"We'll wrap up this morning.

"Good, that will keep us on track. Mr. Mills?"

"At least the rest of today, maybe half of tomorrow your honor."

"Well, let me say this about that, I have been watching this jury and they are getting bored. We need to speed this up. Mr. Mills I will give you until the end of the day to present your case and worst-case scenario will have closing arguments tomorrow morning.

"You're kidding me your honor, aren't you?"

"I never joke Mr. Mills. Do you understand?"

"Judge, there are all sorts of constitutional problems with you forcing me to present my case in such a limited manner. You don't want this do you?" I said looking over to Simms.

Simms chimed in. Judge I can trim my case down to one more witness and close my case in chief. That way, Mr. Mills has the same amount of time that I did.

"Sounds fair to me Mr. Mills. What do you say?" The now smiling robed one said. It was the first time had seen him smile in months.

'I stand by my objection." I said through my resolutely clenched teeth. I needed them both to think I was so screwed. 'I got your screwed' I thought to myself grabbing my crotch in my mind.

"Noted. Lets roll, gentleman. We are wasting valuable court time"

As Simms and I turned back to our desks I pulled him aside. I whispered, "You really want to try this case a third time?" Simms could tell how pissed off I was, from the gravel in my voice.

"You and I may have to try it again, but he won't. He got re-elected just to finish out his pension. Two more years and he are off the bench, retired and sucking rum and cokes in Bimini. He never has to see or hear about Sissy again. And you are just a bad memory. Olst is out of here in eight months. What's that lyric, 'Looks like it's you and me again." Simms did not seem worried about his honor's motive. Truth be known, it sounded like he expected it. Simms and I returned to our desks.

"The Commonwealth calls detective Olst." An obvious choice if you have limited time. Olst reminded me that you can dress a gorilla up in a tuxedo and he's still a gorilla. You can put a gorilla in detective's clothes and he is a gorilla with a badge. Dumber with a badge was a dangerous combination and Olst was proof of this. Olst just had a badge and a 'kill 'em all and let God sort 'em out' mentality. Yet this gorilla had a conviction rate in the ninety-sixth percentile. Like an organ grinder's trained monkey Olst took the oath, looked at Simms and signaled that he was ready. Jurors naturally like cops. Regardless of which branch, of the family tree, man or ape where they came.

"State your name age, occupation and how long you have had that employment" Simms asked robotically. I did not need to hear the preliminaries. I knew Olst's qualifications. I directed my attention to my Polish pal.

"Where is our blonde babe?" I whispered to Kurt

"Damned if I know." He whispered.

"Well you got the wrong person. She is not St. Claire. She faked you out. I want her in my back pocket for the rest of the day. Even if you have to baby-sit her and tell her every cop story you ever made up to impress a bimbo at a bar."

"Now?"

"Before now. The asshole in the robe just cut our courtroom time." Kurt looked shocked. "Don't tell me the constitutional problems, that's my job.

You find that blonde and get her here. I don't care how and I don't want to know how." Then I said like Jack Nicholson in a *Few Good Men*, one of Kurt's top ten trial movies. "We clear?"

"Crystal." He said imitating Tom Cruise. Kurt got up quietly, momentarily distracting Olst. The consummate professional witness, but he quickly turned back to the jury to tell them every answer to Simms' questions. Sissy looked at me wondering where Kurt was going. I brushed it off like it was nothing. The three jurors who noticed Kurt get up and leave returned their attention to Olst. He continued looking in their eyes making sure he had the juror's attention again. After all, people believe someone that looks them in the eye. Problem was, Olst could look you in the eye while pissing on your shoe and convince you it was raining. He even made you feel thankful for the weather report.

What were you doing on the night that Mr. Walker was killed?

"I was the head investigator on duty."

'Yeah, the one with dirty knees.' I thought to myself. My only question was, who was on the receiving end of his voluntary genuflecting? I smiled to myself, because I recognized that whenever I asked and started asking myself a lot of questions I got closer to the answer. A reverse thought process for Simms, but the norm for me.

"Continue." Simms said gesturing to Olst to tell the jury what he had done in a non-stop narrative fashion. Normally, I would object to the narrative form because it gave me no opportunity to object to things he might say, but I decided that if I gave him free reign, he might make a mistake in his testimony.

"When I got the call, I got to the scene as soon as I could. Of course, the deputies that arrived at the scene first, had started interviewing the few witnesses that were there. Mr. Walker had already been taken the hospital. The coroner was there, so I knew that the ambulance was carrying a dead body to the hospital. I asked the coroner if he had notified the family, and he indicated he had not. He was going to go there immediately after he completed his investigation. Not wanting to interfere with his job, I talked to the deputies and found out which of the few witness had the most information. There were two, a Mr. Gaines and a Mr. Brown." Before he could get out their information I jumped in.

"Objection your honor, hearsay."

"Sustained, try not to tell us what others said." He said from behind the bench. Olst knew it was hearsay but tried to get it in anyway, try to see if I was asleep at the wheel.

"What did you do, based on what Mr. Gaines told you."

"I sent a deputy, to Ms. Carol West's home."

" And based on Mr. Brown's statement?"

"I sent another deputy to go find a witness that might have also been in the parking lot at the time the shot was fired."

"And based on that, what happened?"

"We brought Ms. West if for an interview. We could never find the other person, no matter how hard we tried. Like nothing I ever saw. You would think it would be impossible to hide in these days of computers, but that witness did."

"Ever get a artists sketch of that person?"

"Nope sure did not."

"Why not?"

"Just didn't think of it and how do you get a sketch of a shadow? Besides, kind of hard to do with the only one eyewitness gone. We had seen the shooter, seemed like a waste of good police resources.

"How did you find the defendant?"

"Based on what Ms. West told us."

"What did the defendant tell you when you got her to the station?"

Olst proceeded to tell the jury everything; he had at the first trial. This time, with more emphasis where he thought it helped his case. I now stood at the podium taking notes with the transcript from the first trial, trying to find inconsistencies between his testimonies first the first trial and this trial. Emily handed me a note. I reached down and tried not to be seen as I retrieved the note. I opened it up. It read, 'this has still got to be one of the ugliest toupees that I have ever seen! Is he trying to hide his bald head in plain sight?' I held back the smile that was beginning to grow in the left corner of my mouth. She knew when I needed something to pick me up, no matter how serious the occasion. It put things in perspective. I returned my attention to the witness stand concentrated on his testimony. But I scribbled a note back to her. I handed it to her and she opened it. 'No wonder the boys on the force call him Kojak.' I penned on the back of her note. I handed it back to her, noticing for the first time that Sissy and was noticing the repartee that was going on between the two teenagers passing notes back and forth while her life was in the balance. She had to be wondering what was being said between Emily and myself just like she was wondering what was said between Walker and the blonde that night. She did not know what we were writing back and forth just like she did not know how she had killed Walker. It was all taking place right in front of her yet she was missing it. Olst finished his summary of his investigation stating, "We arrested the defendant and charged her with murder. She said, "She did not do it." That she had aimed high. She told us where the gun was because she said the ballistics would show she did not do it. I asked her who else could have fired the shot and she had no answer. We retrieved the pistol and sent it to the lab to the young lady that testified yesterday. "

Recognizing that time was short, Simms tendered Olst for cross-examination. I was amazed. This had to be a record for shortest direct testimony in a murder case.

"When was the last time you were in Evansville, detective?"

"Objection." Simms interrupted, "How does Evansville figure into a case that occurred entirely in the bottoms of McCracken County?

"Sustained. Mr. Mills, Lets keep the case in this jurisdiction."

"I cannot recall if you have ever been in my office, before Detective Olst. Have you?"

"Your honor."

"Fair warning Mr. Mills."

"Have you always worn that ugly toupee, detective?" Half the jurors smiled and the other half chuckled.

The robed wonder, did not need an objection from Simms. I don't remember much about that funny moment, but I do remember 'contempt' coming out of his mouth before his gavel hit the bench. "I will deal with you after this jury is out of my presence. Consider yourself grateful for that Mr. Mills. It will give me much needed time, to cool down."

Emily looked at me, like I had been diagnosed, by a psychoproctologist with terminal cranial rectalitus and needed an emergency removal; if for no other purpose than to make sure the judge had a clear shot at my head when he severed it from my shoulder blades.

Getting back on point and what appeared to be somehow relevant to the case I asked, "You ever find the person that Mr. Brown talked about? A blonde wasn't she? Or did you say? Or again, why waste valuable resources? You had the shooter."

"Oh, is that your theory of the case Mr. Mills?" Olst quipped sarcastically. "You have someone who fired a bullet at Walker, but you don't have the person who pulled the trigger of the gun that discharged the projectile that killed Walker, do you? Got the ballistics or the gun? Got any physical evidence to back up your theory Mr. Mills?""

"We think so."

"I guess 'know so' is the question that the jury has to answer."

"That's how the system works detective. And when it does work it's great isn't it Detective Olst? One last question detective Olst, about Mean Gene the town drunk. Does he still drink Single malt on occasion?" Before Olst could answer the question through his smile I heard a familiar voice.

"That is it, Mr. Mills! The jury is excused until 1:00 p.m. The usual admonition ladies and gentlemen. I will see counsel at my bench, now!"

Olst just smiled, realizing he was not going to be required to answer, that highly irrelevant question. He stepped down from the stand. I walked up to the bench with my best Peter Falk Colombo face, emoting the phrase, 'What? Did I do something wrong'?'

The robed one waited until the last juror left the room, before he came over the bench at me with his invectives."

"You and the Bar Association are about to become intimate friends, Mr. Mills. However, before they have that opportunity, you need to read the rules on relevancy. Bailiff, take Mr. Mills to the jail, bring him back over for the trial ten minutes before it resumes."

"Can't do it your honor."

"Mr. Mills, you mean you can't, you won't, or I can't?"

"Well, judge, actually probably all three. If you jail me now it infringes on my client's right to the effective assistance of counsel in that I will not have access to my notes to prepare her defense. That would result in a mistrial and a reversal and then we do this all over again." Your honor, there is a great line from King Lear, 'There is method to my madness.' I understand my methods and means have been a little, or very unorthodox to your honor, but I now have to wrap my case up within the time constraints you have set, possibly even sooner, if I may remain in the courtroom under the bailiff's 'protection.'

"Bailiff, you stay with Mr. Mills, through the noon recess. He does not leave this courtroom even for a bathroom break without my permission, understand?"

The bailiff nodded. I did the same. Still angry, he waived us away from the bench.

"I will see you all in one hour." I turned and walked away from the bench. When I got back to my desk, I sat down and waited for the judge to leave the room. Then I sat and begged the bailiff to get closer to my ear, and whispered, "Got an empty pocket? He looked at me curiously. "I really got to pee."

If Kurt had been there, he would have shot me, to save me from myself. Sissy was amazed, Emily was wondering, how soon she should start looking for a new job. Her soon-to-be former boss, now either about to be temporarily suspended, from the practice of law or under investigation for mental instability, was on the way out permanently. I leaned into the two of them. They leaned in to me.

"Fortunately for me, this will not be the first time I have made a jackass out of myself in a court room. It will also probably not be the last. "Emily call Kurt and you tell him to get the blonde and have her waiting outside the courtroom at one o'clock sharp. I don't care if he has to kidnap her."

"I got a test for him. If he can not find her and Olst can, he flunks and gets to be embarrassed over the fact that he got out worked by Olst. He won't be able to stand that.

I wonder how long I'm going to put me in jail?" I smirked. Emily and Sissy were not amused. Emily took Sissy's lunch order and took my order for my usual Yoo-hoo. I handed her a twenty to cover the cost. She waived her hand declining.

"You may need that in your canteen account in jail." She was not smiling.

Chapter 39

Life and law have taught me that the perception of reality is reality. If a witness thinks you have evidence you are alluding to, they are more likely to believe that you have the non-existent evidence. So it was with the blonde. Hell, I didn't even know her name. I didn't even have her under subpoena. Had she disappeared, at the order of the powers that be, her sugar-daddy?

The jurors were in their seats promptly at one, amazed to see me in mine. Probably even more amazed to see me still in my suit rather than the usual orange, jail jump suit. Simms had gotten to his seat just before the last juror. He had a front row seat to what was about to be, from his perspective, my last hurrah, or oy-vey, depending on your cultural perspective.

"Call your first witness, Mr. Mills. Your motions for directed a verdict are overruled." I had not even made any such motion, as required by the criminal rules. Perhaps, he thought I was mad and wanted to protect his record.

"Defense calls," I paused, "The defendant, Sissy Gilbert." The look on Sissy's face was indescribable. The only one more amazed was Simms. It was a trademark of my practice that I kept my clients off the stand, and now I was putting her on the stand. What the hell was I thinking, both he and Sissy must have been thinking, if I was thinking at all? Sissy rose and leaned into me.

"Have you lost your mind?" She said with a deliberate pause between the 'your' and 'mind' for emphasis. "I'm not even prepared to testify. You told me I would not have to testify and that my character was horrible and I would be convicted if I took the stand."

"Look Sissy, I have to buy time. Kurt has not found the blonde and there is no one else to put on for our case. Besides, if I have this figured out correctly you testimony is not going to matter. If I've got it wrong, I'll be the first to testify at the hearing on your ineffective assistance of counsel hearing. Besides, if I get it wrong and the golden rule applies you will do time in Peewee Valley anyway."

"Mr. Mills, are you going to let your first witness take the stand or are we going to watch the two of you whisper to each other?" Simms smiled, the jurors chuckled, he spun his gavel in his hand.

"Go ahead, take the stand." She rose to the witness stand, and to everyone's amazement to the occasion. I began with the usual material.

"Sissy, we have all heard everyone talk about you, but Sissy, tell them your name."

"My real name? You really want it, Mr. Mills?"

"Sissy is a nickname?" I asked. The indictment had not even been issued as an a.k.a. Everyone thought her legal name was Sissy. Great time for them to find out. Any other secrets? I wondered.

"Cecilia C. Gilbert. Folks call me Sissy. When we was growing up my little brother couldn't say, Cecelia. He called me Cee-Cee. So the family made it Sissy. I got another secret for you Mr. Mills."

'Oh great', I had no idea what that was going to be and now was not the time to find out, but I was about to. "What's the secret Sissy?"

"Actually, it's no secret. I didn't kill Walker. I may have done a lot of bad things in my life, but I did not kill him. We had our disagreements, but I never wanted to kill him." Great, now I had to find out in front of the jury, what they disagreed about before, Simms asked her.

"What would you disagree about, Sissy?" She looked down, embarrassed before she gave the answer.

"We disagreed over girl friends. Sometimes, we liked the same girl at the same time. We would get jealous of each other. Sometimes I think he did it to me deliberately. He had more power because he had access to drugs and most of our girlfriends liked to get high. I did not have that kind of money. He did."

"Objection, there has been no reference to Mr. Walker as a drug person. Move to strike." Simms said, trying to save a pimp's reputation.

"Judge, there was pot found in Walker's pocket and there were all the drugs that were found in his system by the state pathologist. I think there is a sufficient foundation for the inference that he used drug."

Simms thought about it. "You know judge, I think I can use it to my advantage. I will withdraw the objection." He returned to taking notes at his desk.

"Did you see him get high that night?"

"No, but I could tell from his behavior that he was real high. When he was high he acted real bad. I guess the word is arrogant. Some people get high and they think they are bullet proof, invisible and in, uh, in, what's the word?

"Invincible?"

"Yeah, that's it. That Friday night after Thanksgiving, we ended up interested in the same girl."

"What did she look like Sissy? Did you get her name? Ever see her before?" I begged. "She was a drop dead gorgeous blonde. I mean really, well built. Turned all the young boy's heads. She was talking to Walker a lot but she and I were making a lot of eye contact. I guess you call it 'gay-dar' instead of radar. Like when a straight person knows that another person is interested in them by they way they look at you."

This was clearly more information than, either the blue haired Baptist jurors or the straight red necks like Goball needed. They were clearly turned off and would convict Sissy just became of her sexual proclivity, not because she killed Walker.

I needed to cut to the chase and do some damage control. "Did you and Walker have words outside, The Valley, that night before closing?" She told what happened like a yellow dog democrat recites the party line the night before an election, trying to convict a republican in the error of their ways. She walked all the way through the echo, both sound and light, and to Carol giving her a ride home. "And do you know what caused the second light and sound echo in the grotto?"

"Someone else fired a shot." Simms looked at Sissy and threw his pen onto the table for both its dramatic effect and to express his disbelief.

"Do you know who fired the shot Sissy?"

"Yes I do."

"And who is she?"

"Objection your honor, no foundation, she said he did not see the person, so how can she know?"

"Because Carol West, who gave me a ride home told me." She interjected excitedly. Simms smiled. He had her trapped. She could not support her conspiracy theory and that's all it would be. The jury would be out a record one and a half minutes to a verdict. He looked across the courtroom at me, to see if I had the same appreciation for the moment.

"Then the answer calls for hearsay your honor. It is pure unadulterated rank hearsay, and she can't say what Ms. West told her."

The robed one did not even wait for my answer. He had his ruling made when Simms stood up. "Mr. Mills, if you know of some exception to the hearsay rule that I don't I will have to sustain the objection. Know of any such exception?"

"Not that I can think of right now your honor, but if I do later I'll let you know." It was not a time to be flip, but I had nothing else to say, so I relied on old habits. Sissy looked at me, hanging out on the gangplank, her eyes about to fill up. But she was too tough, and would not give Simms the satisfaction of seeing her cry.

"Ladies and gentlemen of the jury you are admonished to ignore the witness's last statement. It is hearsay and is inadmissible. Can you ignore it?" They all nodded obediently.

"If I may have a moment to look over my notes your honor before I tender the witness for cross?" He nodded his assent. I walked over and looked at a blank piece of paper and whispered to Emily, "How am I doing so far?"

She did not dignify the question with an answer. She was trying too hard not to look disgusted at a man, she had told others she would follow into hell. Now, she didn't even want to be with me on the same side of a courtroom. She looked up and forced a smile, trying to indicate to the jury we knew what we were doing. She never was a very good liar.

"No further questions, your honor." I looked at Simms, tendering Sissy up for his circus act. Sissy, about to do a hire wire act above the jury, three hundred feet in the air, no net below, and we had just figured out that she had not learned to walk yet. I had put Sissy on the stand, to buy time, for Kurt to get back. He was not back and Simms was about to pounce.

If I thought Sissy was shocked when I called her to the stand, it was nothing compared to the look on my face, when Simms approached his podium and made his announcement to the court.

Chapter 40

❖❖ The most difficult thing for a trial attorney to do is shut up. It is not in our nature. We are genetically programmed to question on command, even on the most esoteric of subjects. The fact that we know absolutely nothing about the witnesses field of expertise does not deter us from plunging head first into fifteen minutes of blather, affectionately referred to as cross-examination. Only the most seasoned and secure attorneys have the uncommon sense to announce that they realize that if the witness has not hurt them and they are not going to make any headway with a witness, then announce that they have, "No questions your honor."

I recognized the strategy, and maybe the judge did too. But no one else in the courtroom did. Olst, second chair, and two paralegals were aghast. I had to pick Emily's jaw off the floor. If Kurt had been there I would have had to revive him with smelling salts. But it was, and to this day, remains a very clever move.

The theory- Let Sissy's claim that it was some one else, an unknown person who shot Walker just hang out there. No other witness to support the claim. Absolutely, no corroboration, even The Warren Commission's support would be no help. And besides, West was not going to testify to any such theory. She just drove her home and did not see a second shooter. Simms knew I had to call her next, and she was the witness that would seal the case for the Commonwealth. Hoist, Sissy by her own petards.

"Next witness Mr. Mills." The robed one ordered.

"Carol West, your honor."

'That asshole jailer.' I thought to myself. West had civilian clothes but she was wearing her pumpkin orange county issue jump suit. At least the bailiff knew not to have her in handcuffs when he escorted her to the witness stand. She did the inmate two step, shuffling to the witness stand. She sat, looked at the robed one and raised her right hand without being told to. Jurors expected this of cops. They testified thousands of times. By raising her hand without being told West proved to the jury that this was not her first rodeo.

"You are Carol West." I stated, rather than asking the witness to state her name age and address. I really did not want to ask that last question. No telling what she was going to say, and I had already either created or experienced enough surprises for one day.

"You understand, why you are here today?"

"Yeah, I gave your client a ride home after she shot Walker."

"Well, now let's take this one step at a time. When you testified before the grand jury, you testified that you didn't give her a ride. Then we took your testimony at the last trial, was that you did, give her a ride home. Now which is it?"

"I gave her a ride." She retorted, nonchalantly.

"And what else did you see?"

"Like what?"

To say, I have a short fuse is like saying that the A-Bomb is a firecracker. Like my father, I do not suffer fools lightly. I often realize that the more I wanted to be less like my father, the more I was like him. Sometimes that was not a bad thing. Playing my weaknesses to my strength- emotional dyslexia. When in this spot, I cut to the chase.

"Alright Ms. West, lets get to it. Who has gotten to you?" my voice rising, affirming my discontent."

"Why I don't know what you mean Mr. Mills." Figuring if she did her best southern bell, to my Yankee Jew, she would win.

"The last trial you were falling all over yourself to help Sissy. Even admitted you committed perjury to help us get to the truth. Now you're in a hurry, to get out of here and off the stand. Mr. Simms came and saw you this morning and talked to you didn't he?" Simms could not object because he knew it was true, and if he objected I could call him to the stand to prove it. And he did not want to be the cause of a mistrial by having to testify as a witness, something he knew he could not do. Besides, so he talked to her. Good lawyers, talked to witnesses before they testified all the time.

"Yeah, just after you did." She said. I looked over at Simms. Now this was news to him. I was not even supposed to know that she was in the jail, and I did. How did I know that? More importantly, what had West and I talked about?

"You remember what we talked about?"

"Yeah, about testifying to the truth like I did at the avowal."

"Anything else?"

"Not that I recall?"

"You ever tell Sissy you saw a second shooter, saw who it was that fired the second shot. It was a blonde. You remember any of that from this morning?"

"First time I heard that, Mr. Mills." She glanced over at Simms for approval. He just looked back, expressionless. "You got a mystery shooter, fired the shot? You got a witness up your sleeve?"

"Nope, but you know, they don't search attorney's when they come into jail. When I talked to you in Indiana we were alone. I did not record the conversation in spite of the fact that my P.I told me I should. I did what he told me to do today though. You were on tape. I had my micro-cassette recorder with me. Armed and loaded. Want to hear what you had to say when you did not think you were being recorded?" Before she could answer Simms hit his feet. Before Simms could hit his feet, the robed one had finished the second down stroke of his gavel.

"In chambers. Now Mr. Mills!"

'Holy shit', I thought, 'Whose nerve had I hit first?' I guess I was about to find out.

"Judge, I think we can clear this up at the bench." Simms said, sensing my eminent doom and wanting the jury to witness it. Nothing like a good public hanging to satisfy the masses. A perquisite to the twelve dollars and fifty cents a day they got paid. Twelve easy votes at the next election.

CHAPTER 41

❖ I am glad I followed Kurt's admonition and did what I didn't do at the Vandenberg jail. I plucked the tape recorder and the micro-cassette of my conversation with Carol from my right suit jacket pocket.

"What's that Mr. Mills?" Simms asked.

"It's a tape of my conversation with Carol West this morning."

"Objection your honor."

"Granted Mr. Simms." He did not even wait to hear Simms' grounds, but Simms continued so that the record was clear. Your honor we had no notice of this evidence. Besides, he is going to try to impeach his own witness."

"Just got it this morning your honor. I did not know it was going to be evidence until Ms. West decided to at best, vacillate, and at worst, prevaricate under oath. Perjury if you will."

"It is inadmissible, Mr. Mills and you will get reported to the bar again, and maybe even indicted for wire tapping.

"As long as one party to a conversation consents to the recording it is not wire tapping." I replied. Simms reached for and opened his criminal code. He looked at the statute and scanned the annotations under it. He smiled, realized his opportunity and capitalized on it.

"Your honor, Mr. Mills is correct. I assume since he recorded the conversation that he consented to the recording and therefore it was not illegally recorded. You did consent didn't you Tim?" I smiled my answer. Was he on board?

"How about the surprise?" The robed one asked.

"We waive it, in the interest of justice. I'm interested in Mr. Mills' theory now. It's been implied that I am some-how implicated in a cover up of this murder, and this may be an opportunity to clear the air, at least as far as my reputation is concerned." I knew Simms was out now.

"Any other problems, your honor?" I asked with a smirk.

"A ten minute recess, gentlemen. I have to look at the statute and bar rules myself. I will see both of you in exactly ten minutes. Exactly!" We walked out, having dismissed from our audience with exalted one.

"Ok. My Jewish dyslexic Yankee colleague. What you got?"

"You think there is really something on that tape? That would be illegal."

Now, he was really confused. Not even I had the balls to pull off a bluff like this. I smiled. "Of course it's on there. Now we just have to find out the person that told the shooter to pull the trigger. I have go get a drink of water. I'm supposed to drink as much water as possible to help this gout. I walked out into the hall to get a drink from the water fountain. My tall Polish friend was there. He had company.

When the ten minutes were up. Simms and I walked into chambers. As I had asked, Simms brought Olst in with him. I turned to Simms, "Mr. Simms, could you ask Detective Olst to hand you his cell phone?" Simms held his hand out. Initially Olst resisted. Simms just hardened his look and Olst complied. Olst did not want to get into that power play. He did not bring anything to the table in that game.

"Now press star 69 and see what number pops up." He complied.

"Recognize it?" Simms nodded.

"Judge, would you honor us by doing the same with your phone?"

"I don't have that application on my phone Mr. Mills. It keeps curious people like you from invading the sanctity of this office. Is this what you have Mr. Mills."

"No judge. A tape, a cell phone, a large polish person and his date. May I introduce his date?" I asked rhetorically. I nodded to the bailiff to bring Kurt in. In walked Kurt with the blonde.

"Any need for introductions your honor, detective Olst?"

"You know detective, when you are in a whole, quit digging. There may be a dyslexic, Jew standing outside the hole throwing the dirt back, in on you. You looked in my office for something, that did not exist. The more you looked for it the more interested I became. But who had you digging? Only one person, Olst, you forget that when in a conspiracy that when a co-conspirator commits an act not envisioned by the original conspiracy, you are just as culpable. You never envisioned that the drug buy would involve murder."

"It was a controlled buy. That is what I'll testify to, it went bad and by her own actions Walker got shot."

"No good Olst. You weren't there to monitor the buy. You showed up later to do the investigation. Protocol requires you to be within two miles of the bust. You were at the station. You got involved in this crap, after the fact. Anything else bugging you Olst? He was getting the fact, that I was now making a pun.

I looked at the blonde. "Nice catch Kurt. I don't want to know how you found her, but you did. Simms, I'm happy Kurt works for the good guys. Pay ain't great but the satisfaction is out of sight."

"You're right about that counselor. You don't want to know how I got her and the pay ain't great"

"Young lady. All this started, because you and your lover wanted some drugs for a good time. Why you decided to kill Walker, will have to come out another time. I'm not too concerned with the why right now. I know the what and when. I just need one more who, along with you. Not too many people can get you second, or even a third ID. access to the clerk's office and favors. It must be a really powerful person. She looked down. Then she looked down and looked to Olst for direction.

"I think this young lady needs her Fifth Amendment rights read to her Mr. Mills." The judge said.

"Or I can make her a deal right here and now your honor. Something involving immunity perhaps. What do you think young lady?" Simms said, piquing her interest now. Simms wanted to know the 'who' and he would do anything to find out. But first we had to discuss Sissy's fate.

"You'll excuse us your honor, we have to discuss Ms. Gilbert's case." He nodded understandably.

Chapter 42

❖❖ Protection comes in various forms. Sexually its condoms or diaphragms. For prosecutors, it's qualified immunity and for judge's absolute immunity that keeps them from getting screwed. Sims and I walked out of the judge's chambers to discuss settling Sissy's case. Time served was not a choice for me even if Sissy would take the deal. We didn't walk down to his office. Instead we stood outside the judge's chamber door. Simms put his index finger to his lips. He leaned toward the door and motioned for me to do the same. I leaned in.

"You doing O.K?" the judge asked.

"I'm hanging in there." A female voice responded.

Evidently, Kojack sat there like the bump on the log he was, saying nothing, at least we couldn't hear him say anything.

Turning to Olst he said, "You keep your mouth shut about what you did at Mills office for me, if you ever want one of your paper thin search warrants to withstand a motion to suppress."

Simms looked at me for a reaction. I gave him none. I could tell he was debating whether or not to go back into the judge's chambers and let them know what we had heard or just wait to see if they were going to say anything else. They did.

"Will I see you tonight?" The judge asked

"Do you think it will be safe?" She replied. "Will there be any warrants for you to sign tonight? We still have 'friends' out there that need to know that."

Simms had all even he could stand. He opened the door and answered the question for her. "Probably not."

The judge did not miss a beat. "Mr. Mills, based on the fact that I am going to rule the tape inadmissible, and your second shooter theory is an aphorism, a ghost, I suggest your client consider a plea agreement."

Simms looked at me and then at the three of them. "I think I've got an offer that Tim will take judge. The Commonwealth will move to dismiss the charges against Sissy. I'll be asking the next grand jury to indict the cute blond lady, under her real name and all a.k.a.'s for murder, obstruction of justice, tampering with evidence, and anything else I can think of between now and then. You, your honor, you go down for, at a minimum for just plain old obstruction, destruction of evidence, tampering with a witness, accessory to burglary, and anything I can think of between now and the time I walk back into my office to get a warrant for your arrest. Of course, signed by the judge, from the other division, He dare not sign it for fear that by not signing it would mean he was involved too. I don't need to make a deal for you either detective, or about to be 'former' detective Olst. Will I, Olst?"

"Kojak, we indict you on a burglary, arson first, intimidating a witness, tampering with physical evidence. Judge, Olst will roll over on you. Count on it! Cops are really persona-non-gratis in prison. Solitary confinement is a tough way to do time, isn't it Kojak?

Judge, you don't have to worry about your pension. I hear the penitentiary has a great pension plan- three hots and a cot. I'm sure the defendants you sentenced so compassionately will be looking forward to your arrival. Protective custody is nice, but a bit isolated. Maybe you and Kojack will be cellmates.

Simms pulled out his cell phone and tapped the three digits for nine-eleven. "This is Simms, send up four of your best deputies. I've got three going to lock up. Oh yeah, tell them to tell the jailer to put them all on suicide watch. Wouldn't want to lose them before trial. We won't need a bailiff for Sissy, she'll be walking out of the jail in a couple of minutes. The deputies arrived. Simms gave them the details so they could arrest them all.

Simms turned to me. "I'll have to get a special prosecutor since I'll be a witness to what we just heard. Tim, stick around. I'll want to get a statement from you before you leave the courthouse so we have your testimony, by avowal so to speak, just to be sure nothing happens to you. Something about you being in your office when the arson took place leads me to believe that there may be some more charges out of this. Don't you think so, judge?" The judge sat there silently. "I take it from your silence your honor that you understand you Miranda rights."

I walked back into the courtroom. Everybody in the jury watched as I sat back down next to Sissy. Simms came in. The judge from the other division came in and dismissed the jury. The jury looked shocked. I looked at Goball. He was speechless. Emily heard the words come from the judge's mouth. She did not know what had happened, but knew that dismissing the panel was good thing. Sissy did not understand what was happening.

"You remember whet I told you my second most favorite word in the world was that started with "F" and ended in "K"?

"Yeah, that was real cute." She said, "It was 'fork'"

"You remember what my favorite four letter word was that started with the letter "F" was?" Sissy looked at me, thought for a second back to that discussion in jail and said, "Free?"

"Yeah, Sissy, Free." I said.

Chapter 43

❖ Every now and then, the legislature gets it right. The entire Commonwealth was outraged about the events, the trials, and more particularly, the robed one, the cop and the blonde. Criminal actions, by the judge were absolutely not covered by his absolute immunity. It may have covered his activity on Kojack's warrant activities, but that was someone else's worry. Sissy had given up years of her life needlessly. Her lost wages were meager. Her lost time, in terms of her overall life expectancy, was not that great. But the public outcry screamed for both punitive and apologetic measures. The legislature, as a body as a whole, felt the outcry, and unanimously passed "Sissy's Bill', compensating Sissy for the injustice done to her and her family. Fortunately, the legislature did not measure her loss by the cost of her attorney's fees. But they did make it all for pain and suffering, so none of it was taxable. By the time 'Sissy's Bill' had made its way through the process a large six figure check was on the Commonwealth's Treasurer's desk.

A month after the legislative session ended Sissy came into my office without an appointment. Sissy and Emily hugged before I knew Sissy was there. They came through my office door, Sissy still smiling from seeing Emily. She didn't cover her mouth. She had had her teeth fixed, capped or crowned. She had put on at least twenty pounds. She didn't say anything. She just walked up to me, put her arms around my neck and started to cry. I joined her.

"We come a long ways together, didn't we, Mr. Mills?"

"You, a whole lot further than me, Sissy."

"We did a lot of it together, though."

"That we did Sissy, that we did."

"You put me before the money. Some said you get it backwards, putting' justice before money, like that readin' problem you told me you had or still got. If you still got it I sure am glad, because no one else saw my case the way you did." She leaned forward and reached into her back pocket and pulled something out.

She handed me an envelope. I didn't even look at the envelope. To look inside while she was there would have been gauche and demeaning. Whatever the amount, it would be fine.

"The numbers on the check in this envelope ain't backwards Mr. Mills. Thanks, is still thanks, whether you figured it out from front to back, or vers-a-visa.

THE END